JJ WEATHERILL

Promoted and Dead

First published by Weatherill Essentials - Publishing 2024

Copyright © 2024 by JJ Weatherill

All rights reserved. No part of this publication may be reproduced, stored or transmitted in any form or by any means, electronic, mechanical, photocopying, recording, scanning, or otherwise without written permission from the publisher. It is illegal to copy this book, post it to a website, or distribute it by any other means without permission.

This novel is entirely a work of fiction. The names, characters and incidents portrayed in it are the work of the author's imagination. Any resemblance to actual persons, living or dead, events or localities is entirely coincidental.

This ebook file is rights protected and can not be reproduced, copied or sold by any party other than the publisher or author.

First edition

ISBN: 9798883383211

This book was professionally typeset on Reedsy. Find out more at reedsy.com

This book is dedicated to Dallas Weatherill, the love of my life. He took me in while I found myself and gave me the strength to let the world know that I can be a strong, independent woman. I am so excited to be marrying him in April of 2024 and beginning this new CHAPTER of my new life wrapped in his arms.

Contents

Acknowledgments	ii
MAP & KEY	iii
CHARACTERS	v
Prologue	vii
1 Evil Comes To Town	1
2 No Vacancy	8
3 Promoted & Dead	16
4 Friends & Lovers	23
5 Mama Bear Awakens	29
6 Exchange Of Information	40
7 Sabotage?	48
8 Sleuth Loralin Rides at Dawn	61
9 Emotional Rollercoasters	78
10 Who To Trust	88
11 The Three Musketeers Go To The City	97
12 Bread & Milk	109
13 Murder & Mint-Chip Ice Cream	124
14 Surveillance Expert Loralin Robbins	152
15 Gunshot Wounds, Love, & Other Things	159
16 It's A Family Affair	173
Epilogue	187
About the Author	189

Acknowledgments

I want to thank my ex-husband and my kids for their support in my writing for so long. I couldn't have started this career without them and I love them very much.

I want to thank my Australian family, Matthew, Kristy, Tycan, DJ, and Sebastian for all of the love, support, and kindness they showed to me when I showed up on their doorstep needing a place to stay. I will never be able to thank you enough.

I want to thank my friend Betty for giving me the love of Cozy Mystery that led to these books.

I want to thank my friend Kelly for all of the support she's given to me not only in writing but in my personal life too.

I want to thank my beta readers, author friends, irl friends, and my family for their unwavering support now and in the past.

MAP & KEY

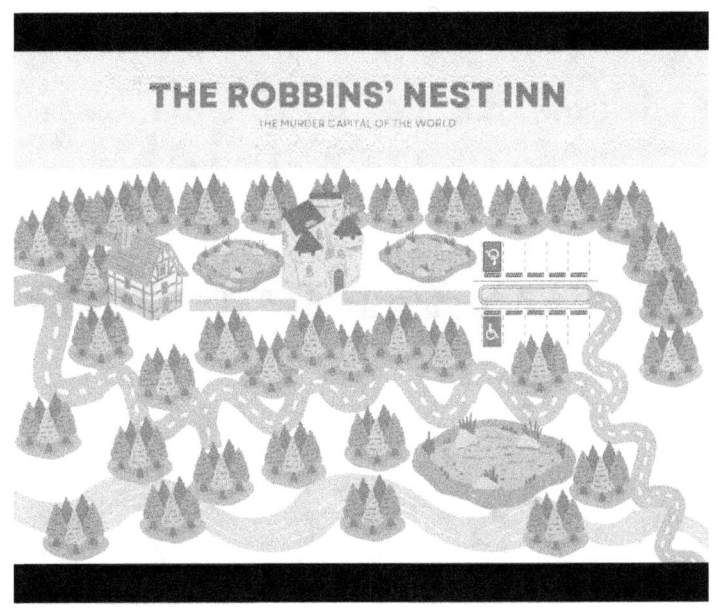

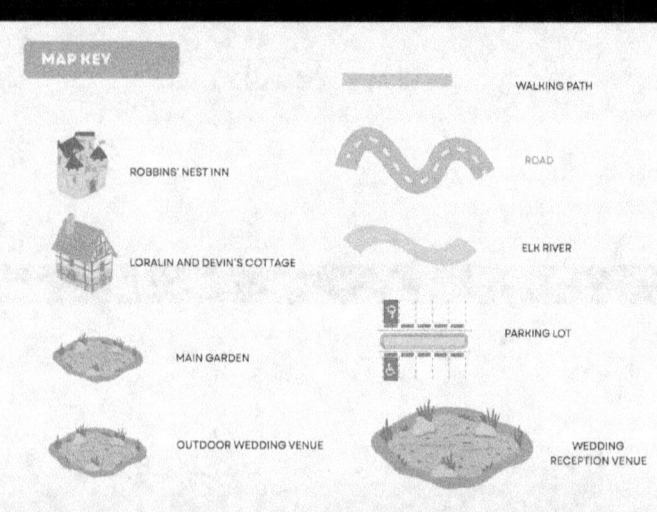

CHARACTERS

MAIN CAST

Loralin Robbins - *51 years old. Inherited the Inn from her grandparents and decided to renovate and reopen after years of being closed down. Best Friends with Devin Wentworth*

Devin Wentworth - *25 years old. Helped his parents run their hotel in Tasmania, Australia. Decides to move to America to escape his family and help Loralin run the Inn. Best Friend to Loralin Robbins.*

Miles Robbins - *51 Years old. Detective for the Elk River Police Department. Ex-husband of Loralin Robbins. He's a stereotypical short-statured, middle-aged 'local cop'.*

SUPPORTING PLAYERS

Phyllis Palmer - *50 years old. New Head Labor and Delivery nurse at Natrona County Medical Center. Hates Loralin and Miles and their kids. Hated by the whole town and almost everyone she works with. Chef Pierre's ex-wife.*

Deke Robertson - *Mid 50s. Hotel owner known for using devious and illegal ways to take over existing hotels. Bane of Loralin's* *existence. Hated by pretty much everyone.*

Mark and Trevor Wentworth - *47 and 12 years old. Devin's father and brother, who decided to stay on in America. Mark becomes the inn's gardener/handyman.*

Meredith Robbins - *50 years old. Freelance caterer. For her, cooking is life. Miles' new wife. Friends with her husband's ex.*

Heather Robbins - *25 years old. Labor and Delivery Nurse at Natrona County Medical Center. Loralin and Miles' oldest daughter. Devin's ex-girlfriend.*

Hanna Robbins Buchanan - *22 years old. Married to Matthew Buchanan. Lives in Evanston, WY. Loralin and Miles' youngest daughter. Works in IT.*

Chef Pierre Marqui - *In his 70s. Chef of the Inn's Restaurant. Known for his temper. There's something fake about him.*

Lisa Marie and Chloe - *Early 40s. Housekeepers at the inn. Frenemies with Chloe. Lisa Marie dates Devin in an age-gap relationship.*

Don Peterson - *51 years old. Known as Handsy Don because he is known for being annoying in his pursuit of love. Chief of Police in Cheyenne, Wyoming.*

Prologue

Whispers in the room created a flood of noise that ended abruptly when labor and delivery nurse Phyllis Palmer entered. Anyone familiar with the hospital knew that the whispers had been about her, their own Nurse Ratched. Phyllis was known as the meanest, pettiest woman to ever live on the planet Earth.

Heather Robbins sat in the meeting room at Natrona County Medical Center as the labor and delivery nurses awaited the announcement of who their new head nurse would be. When Tanner Healthcare took over the hospital, the previous head, Donna, had quit and gone to work for a doctor two states away. Now, Phyllis Palmer was up for a promotion to the position, and Heather and her fellow nurses had joined together to try to prevent it. Today, they would know for sure if their plan had worked.

"Can I have your attention?" came from a man in a suit who walked into the room after Phyllis. His name was Jack, and he was from Tanner Healthcare's corporate office. He was the one who held their futures in his hands. "Today I will be announcing all promotions and staff changes that will take effect immediately."

Heather wasn't the least bit interested in what happened elsewhere in the hospital. She knew and approved of the higher-ups who had been moved around or promoted the day Tanner took over. The new head of Neurosurgery or

Orthopedics didn't concern her. She only cared if Phyllis would be in charge of her career. Unfortunately for Heather, her father had chosen her mom over Phyllis in high school. Since that day, the bitter woman hadn't said one nice thing to anyone related to Loralin and Miles Robbins.

"And now, last but not least," Jack said, shifting his papers on the podium. "The new Head Nurse of Labor and Delivery will be Phyllis Palmer."

The silence in the room was immediate, thick, and suffocating to Heather. Without waiting to hear anyone's reactions, she stood up and left the room. "This can't be happening," she heard herself murmur.

"Can someone kill that bitch already?" she heard coming from behind her. Apparently, she wasn't the only one who had left the room. By the time she made it to the end of the hall and turned around, every labor and delivery nurse was there.

"What are we going to do?" she asked.

"I have no idea," her friend Jenny said softly. "I don't know if I can work for her. We could always find ways around her crap when she was one of us. But she's the boss now."

Heather reached out and touched her friend's arm. "I know. Why the hell…" Just then, Jack walked past them, and she moved away from Jenny to follow him. "Jack. Can I speak to you for a moment?"

"Sure, Heather," he said with a sigh. "What's up?"

"Why the hell did you guys promote her? After her record, after all of our complaints…?" Heather felt like crying, but she would never do it in front of that corporate yahoo.

"Because she was the most qualified and we didn't want to have to do a search for a qualified head."

"Right," Heather huffed. "And how much money did that

save you? In the end, she's going to cost you even more with all the lawsuits from her incompetence. You probably didn't even look over all of the proof we gave you that she is actually *not* qualified."

"I'm sorry," Jack said, even though he sounded more joyous than sorry. "Corporate did what they thought was best. It's done now. It's time to move on."

The rest of the labor and delivery nurses had gathered around by then. "Yeah, maybe it is time to move on. For all of us. And then you can have Phyllis take care of all the patients."

"If you want to leave, Lois. You're more than welcome to." He turned and marched down the hallway and out of the building.

The Labor and Delivery crew stood around and talked for a bit longer until Phyllis walked out of the meeting room. They all then hurried off to the locker room.

Heather grabbed her stuff from her locker and headed out to the parking lot with her phone in her hand to call her mother when Phyllis stepped out in front of her. "Can I help you?" she asked the older woman.

"I just wanted to have a chat," Phyllis cackled.

"About what, Phyllis? I need to call my mother and get home."

"Oh, is little Heather going to cry to mommy that she didn't get her way?" Phyllis oozed pettiness. "I know you were in charge of trying to keep me from getting promoted. So now, it's my turn to repay the favor. I've rearranged the schedule. You'll be working the graveyard shift until further notice."

Heather didn't even have time to think of a comeback before Phyllis was at her car and shut the door. "Stupid bitch," she snarled. "I hope you crash and burn."

"I'm sure you're not the only one," came a deep, kind voice from behind her. "That woman is something else. Have a good night, Heather."

"Uh, yeah, goodnight, Doctor Marshall."

1

Evil Comes To Town

Loralin Robbins stood by the roaring, rushing Elk River where it cut through the property of the Robbins' Nest Inn. Everything seemed to be normal, the singing of the birds was once again loud, and the sense of peace she always seemed to get at exactly this spot washed over her for the first time in a long time.

Just a few months before, she'd opened the Inn to rave reviews and the murder of her head housekeeper. Now, the aftermath was waning, and she was more than ready to get things back on track. Her lifelong dream of reopening her grandparents' Inn was no longer hampered by a dead body, police cars, and crime scene tape.

"Loralin?" came the voice of her best friend, Devin Wentworth. He was also the Inn's manager and over twenty years younger than her. "Is everything okay? I left you out here an hour ago. When you didn't come right back, I got worried."

Loralin turned to the young man who meant the world to her and smiled. "Sorry, I didn't realize I'd been out here this long. It's the first time I've enjoyed this spot in a few months."

"I know," he said, returning her smile. "But we should get back. The guests for the Hospital's promotion party have been arriving."

Loralin turned and walked to where he stood. "I wish we hadn't booked this."

"Hey, at least you get to see your daughter," Devin reminded her over the roar of thunder around them. Heather Robbins had shown up at the inn ahead of all the other celebrants from the hospital.

Loralin looked to the sky. "It's gonna be a bad storm. We'd better get back quick."

"How can you tell?" Devin asked above another roll of thunder.

"Years of living through bad spring storms," she hollered back as she ran through a plot of long spring grasses. "Come on, slowpoke! You're going to want to be inside when this one hits."

"I'm not afraid of a little rain, Loralin!" Devin wanted to stay there, near the river, and watch the rain renew the already fresh spring air.

"You will be when you drown!" she hollered, grabbing his hand and pulling him along. "These storms are nothing to mess with."

The tone of her voice made Devin finally pick up speed to match pace with Loralin. "Are they really that bad?"

"Yep. Just give it a minute." She leaped onto the porch, dragging Devin behind her.

Devin jumped out of his skin at the sound that came from outside after the Inn's double doors closed. "What the hell?" He spun around and his sight set on the window.

"I told you," Loralin said with a chuckle.

"You can't see anything. The visibility is worse than a blizzard," Devin marveled.

"What would you know about blizzards?" Loralin asked with a laugh. She knew he had zero experience with snow. Yet.

"Nothing," he whispered as he stared out the window. "But I know plenty about rain, and I don't think I've ever seen anything like this." When he turned to look at Loralin, he became concerned by the look on her face.

"Oh man, this isn't good," she said, turning to meet his gaze. "If this keeps up, we could have our twenty-year flood today. And since we're in the higher part of town, we might be called on to help."

"We will," came Chef Pierre's voice as he walked up behind the two. "My knee told me loud and clear a couple of hours ago."

"I thought you were leaving, so you didn't have to be here when your ex-wife showed up," Loralin said, referring to a conversation she'd had with the chef who drew people from all over the region to the inn's restaurant for his amazing food.

"I was," he huffed. "But my knee jammed up on the way to the car. I was forced to stay."

"So," Devin asked, butting in. "Your knee jamming up tells you there's a storm?"

"Not at all, young man," the chef said with a hearty laugh. "It tells me when we're going to have a twenty-year flood. The first was when I was ten. The Second was when I was thirty, and the third was when I was fifty. I turn seventy in two days."

Devin was about to say something to the old chef when the man's face went pale, and he turned slowly. "That's my call to leave," he murmured and took off toward the kitchen with his head ducked.

"Loralin! Loralin! Loralin Robbins! Where are you?"

"Would it be wrong if I ran away with Chef Pierre?" she mumbled to Devin as she turned and walked toward Phyllis Palmer. "What can I do for you, Phyllis?"

"How are you holding up, dear? You look a little aged," Phyllis said in her snotty voice, which was also her regular voice.

"Holding up since what, Phyllis?" Loralin's sigh was indicative of the annoyance she was feeling.

"You know, since the divorce," Phyllis whispered.

Loralin laughed. "Miles and I divorced five years ago, Phyllis. I'm over it." She took a long look at her nemesis, who stood way too close to her. "You're the one who never got over Miles."

"You bitch!" she snarled. "How dare you…"

"Hello," Devin said, stepping up to the two women, close enough that Phyllis took a step back.

"Well," Phyllis said, putting her hand to her heart. "Who is this gorgeous specimen, Loralin dear?"

The last thing she wanted to do was introduce the two, but her grandmother had always taught her that politeness came first. "Devin Wentworth, this is Phyllis Palmer, Heather's supervisor. Phyllis, this is the inn's manager, Devin."

Phyllis's look went from bored to interested almost immediately. "Well, now I know why you look so worn out. I think this young man could wear me out." She turned to Devin. "Want to try, gorgeous?"

Devin's face went bright red. "I, umm, I have a girlfriend," he stammered.

"Oh, now come on," she purred. "You could probably handle both Loralin and me."

Now it was Loralin's turn to flush red, only hers was because of anger. "Phyllis Palmer, shut your trap. Devin is dating Lisa

Marie, not me, and why the hell are you out here instead of with your party?"

"Touchy, touchy," Phyllis said. "I came out here to ask for some more cocktail napkins."

"I'll have one of the housekeepers bring some."

Phyllis nodded her head and turned to leave. "You know, everybody in town knows he's your lover. You've always been such a slut, Loralin."

"You stupid bitch," Loralin seethed quietly. "Get the fu…"

"Whoa," Devin cut in, wrapping his arm around her shoulders. "Let's not let the guests hear you talking to a customer like that."

Loralin was able to stop herself and walk back over to the window. "I hate that woman. I wish she would just leave town for good. I had such high hopes when she went away to college."

Devin couldn't help but laugh. "She seems a bit uptight but not overly mean."

"Just wait," Loralin said, looking at him like he'd grown a second head. "That woman could piss off a saint."

"Are you calling me a saint?" he asked to lighten the mood.

"Hardly," Loralin teased back. "But you'll get plenty of chances to do some good deeds today."

They both turned to look back out the window. The rain had slowed, but only a bit. It was still pouring down, and the thunder and lightning were raging.

* * *

Loralin sat behind her desk but didn't relax. She knew better than to get comfortable right now.

"How long before we'll know if it's going to flood?"

"Any time n…" She didn't get a chance to finish her sentence when her cell phone rang. "Hello, Miles."

Her ex-husband's voice was accompanied by the sound of howling wind and pounding rain. She put him on speaker. "Hey, Loralin, we have some stranded motorists who need a warm place to go. And Unit 7 has some locals that need somewhere also. They are closest to you."

"We've got warmth and food. Send them on over." She put her phone into her pocket and sprang up from her chair. Devin knew she was an active person and could get the job done when needed, but he'd never seen this whirlwind side of her. She sure knew how to take charge.

"Lisa Marie," Loralin hollered to one of the housekeepers. "We need all available extra blankets, towels, and robes down in the lobby. Steven, tell Chef we've got incoming, and we need warm, hearty meals! Devin, I need you to call Maureen and see if you can get her in here to help, then we'll go down into the basement and bring up anything that can be used as a place to sit."

Loralin was about to head to the basement door when Phyllis stopped her. "What on earth is going on, Loralin? They interrupted our party!"

"It's flooding, and we are going to be one of the shelters," Loralin said as she opened the door.

"Really? On the day of our celebration? We were here first!"

"Oh, that's right, Phyllis," Loralin said with an exaggerated gasp. "We'll let people be homeless and stranded out in the rain so you can celebrate your promotion. What on earth was I thinking?" She turned and headed down the stairs. When she hazarded a look back, Phyllis was standing there with her mouth wide open and a blush coloring her cheeks.

2

No Vacancy

In no time, the lobby of the Robbin's Nest Inn looked more like a shelter than a country inn. Chairs and unused beds were scattered throughout the space, and piles of linens were stored behind and on the check-in counter. Hot coffee and tea were brewing from the drink kiosk that always stood in the far corner of the room. And one of the waiters rushed out with pots of hot water to set on the warmers along with various flavor packets of hot cocoa.

Loralin was standing behind the counter when she heard the roar of the storm as it entered the building from the opening double doors. "It's show time," she said to Devin. "Let's go greet our guests."

Unit seven brought in two small families, and Miles was right behind them with ten stranded motorists. "Is this all?" Loralin asked her ex.

"No. We have a few more. Do you think you could spare someone to help us sandbag areas that might be hit as the waters flow through the area?"

"If Loralin can handle things here, I'd be glad to come help,"

Devin offered.

"Do you have rain boots and a jacket by chance?" Miles asked the young man he'd become so fond of.

"Yes, sir. I'll run and grab them and meet you back here."

Once Devin was gone, Loralin looked seriously at her ex-husband. "So, how bad is it?"

"So far, we're okay locally. Just people in the gully were affected. And all the humans and pets from that area have been accounted for. You have two of the families here, and the rest were able to get to higher ground themselves. We aren't sure about Antler Acres yet, but flood waters are headed in that direction. Unfortunately, the freeway and the old highway are washed out, so nobody will be able to get to or from Casper for a few days."

Loralin was relieved to hear that, but there was something Miles wasn't telling her. "Spill it, Miles."

He sighed and looked her straight in the eyes. "We had one family get caught in the floodwaters. We weren't able to rescue them before…"

"Damn," Loralin whispered. "Be safe and keep my manager safe, please. I kinda love having him here instead of 8900 miles away."

"Will do," Miles said, smiling at his ex-wife. "Let Heather know she'll have to stay here instead of at my place tonight. They are putting out a no-unnecessary-travel advisory until flood waters fully recede."

Loralin bid farewell to Miles and Devin and turned back to help the people who had come in. For the most part, everyone was just wet and cold. But there were a few scrapes, cuts, and bruises, and possibly one sprained ankle. Without a second thought, Loralin went over to the meeting room where the hospital celebration was taking place and let herself in. Phyllis Palmer was giving a speech.

"Excuse me!" Loralin hollered and watched Phyllis's face pinch with frustration and anger. "We are going to need some doctors and nurses out here to help our flood victims. Could you spare a few?"

"The party is almost over," Phyllis snarled. "You can wait until I'm done!"

Loralin noticed the change in the partygoers to Phyllis's decree. No one seemed surprised that she was more worried about her speech being interrupted than about the natural disaster happening just outside the doors.

Heather was the first one to stand up. "I made a vow as a nurse to help people when needed, not to wait until my boss was done hogging the spotlight." She headed out the door past her mother. All of the other medical personnel quickly followed with a mumbled agreement to Heather's statement.

Phyllis and Loralin were left standing there, glaring at each other and ignoring the sprinkling of hospital administrators who were still in the room. "How dare you!" Phyllis growled until she heard one of her bosses clear their throat. She was only momentarily flustered. "We'll finish this later."

"Remember," Loralin whispered as the other woman slipped past her.

"You're on my turf now."

***

Loralin stood back and looked at the chaos surrounding her. According to reports coming in from Miles' men, the rescue operation was over, and clean-up would begin as soon as daylight hit. The only question now was where on earth her ex-husband and Devin were. They should have been back already.

The big double doors at the entrance of the inn swept open, letting in the now quiet sounds of the night. Miles and Devin stood side by side. Loralin rushed over and hugged the man she'd been waiting to see. "Thank goodness you're okay," she said. Where were you guys?"

"Let me get out of this gear," he breathed heavily. "Then we'll talk."

There was something in his eyes that scared Loralin. What had gone on out there? She needed to talk to Miles. When she turned to where she'd seen him last, he was gone. He was now gathering those who could be taken home and reassuring those who would be sheltering there for a night or two. He didn't look so good either.

"Hey," Devin said, walking up behind her. "Anything I can do to help?"

"You can tell me why you look like you just saw a ghost while you help me sort out rooms for our surprise guests." She dragged him over behind the check-in counter.

"I've never seen someone die before," he murmured as he pulled up the reservation screen on the computer. "Let alone hold someone as they took their last breath."

"What?" Loralin gasped. "Who?"

"Ol' Mrs. Porter," Miles said as he joined them at the counter. "Damn fool woman chased after her shi tzu right into the flood waters. She couldn't keep her balance and..." Miles sighed and shook his head.

Loralin was momentarily stunned by grief. Mrs. Matilda

Porter was the great-granddaughter of the town's founder, a beloved former mayor, and a former elementary teacher to a majority of the kids in town from the sixties to the eighties.

"I waded in after her and carried her to safety," Devin Murmured. "But she didn't make it. She said her dog's name with her last breath."

Loralin took a deep breath and squared her shoulders. "The town is going to be devastated. She was the last of her kind."

The conversation about Mrs. Potter abruptly ended, and Miles left to help load people into the police vans that would take them home. Loralin and Devin quietly set those who were stranded up in rooms, and by dinner time, everyone had a place to lay their tired heads.

* * *

Chef Pierre spent his time trying to cook while also avoiding his ex-wife, Phyllis. It seemed she liked to torture him as much as she did everyone else. Loralin followed the loud, shrill voice of her nemesis as it wafted out of the kitchen. It was apparent that she was making Chef flustered, and Loralin was not going to put up with that. There were too many people who needed to eat that night. "Phyllis, leave him alone, you old crone. He's trying to work."

"Loralin," she sighed. "This is a private conversation."

"Get the Hell out of my kitchen!" Both Chef Pierre and Loralin screamed with the perfect matching pitch and tone. For once, Phyllis had the good grace to look embarrassed as she put her head down and ducked out of the room.

Loralin followed a few seconds behind her and nearly ran

into her daughter in the process. "Heather dear, what's wrong?"

"The big bosses are now insisting that we have to room together with others from the hospital while we're stuck here. something about a surprise free corporate retreat." The young woman was near tears.

"Free my ass," Loralin huffed. "I'll go tell them I'll charge for every minute!"

Heather reached out and grasped her mother's arms in her hands. "Don't, Mama. It will just cause problems. I guess it won't kill me to sleep in the same room as Phyllis for one night."

Loralin pulled her youngest in for a hug. "Are you sure?"

"Yeah," Heather murmured, breaking the embrace.

"Alright, dear, but if it gets too bad, just come to the house, and I'll charge them twice the normal rate if they say anything about it."

"Thanks, Mom. I'm going to go grab a bite to eat. Pray that I don't kill Phyllis overnight."

Loralin gave her daughter a reassuring smile and turned to head back into the kitchen to make sure things were back to normal now that Phyllis was gone. This time, she nearly ran into her ex-husband. "I thought you'd be gone by now."

"No, I wanted to see if you need anything before I head home to check on my wife and the boy."

"I think we're good," Loralin said with a smile. She was so glad that she and her ex still got along most of the time and still genuinely cared about each other. "We have all the supplies we need, and everyone seems to be settling in."

"Good, good. So, what was this about our daughter killing Phyllis?" he said, turning to look at his second-born, who was now stuck at a dinner table with stuffy hospital admin types.

"She just told me to pray that she didn't kill her. They have to be roomies tonight."

"Well, that's just ridiculous. Surely, she's just going to stay with you." It was hard to tell if the look on Miles' face was one of anger or if he was just puzzled.

"Hospital bigwigs are insisting that all hospital employees room together while they are stuck here so they can have a free impromptu corporate retreat." Loralin even felt stupid saying it.

"As I said," Miles harumphed. "Ridiculous. I'm going to head out. Let me or the station know if you need anything."

"Will do. Call or text Devin or me when you get home so we know you made it safely. Some of the streets near your place are bound to still have a lot of water."

"I will," he said before turning around and walking from the room.

Loralin looked around her and decided that the kitchen must be running smoothly because everyone was enjoying dinner and talking animatedly about the adventures of the day. Instead of checking on the Chef and his people, she was going to eat something herself after she found Devin.

"Hey," came the voice she wanted to hear. "There's a table over in the corner. Join me for dinner?"

Loralin turned around and took the hand he offered. "I'm just now realizing how hungry I am. I skipped lunch and only had half a bagel and coffee for breakfast."

"Same," he said as they sat and waved their new head waiter, Steven, over. "I think it's going to be dinner and early bed for just about everyone tonight, including me."

Once their food was ordered, Loralin served up another possibility. "Unless I can talk you into coming to my room to wind down and watch a show or two," she said. For some reason, she wanted him close. The events of the day had thrown her off. There were four people dead, and everyone's lives were upended. She needed some good old-fashioned quality time with Devin and his quiet acceptance of her.

"I could probably go for that. Dinner, a shower, and TV with my bestie. I'm game."

Steven nearly dropped the drinks he'd brought over. "I umm. Here you go." He hurried off in the direction of the kitchen to retrieve their food.

"What was that all about?" Devin asked as Loralin chuckled.

"Steven thinks we are taking a shower *and* watching TV together."

"Bloody Hell! That's not what I meant."

"We both know that," Loralin said, her laughter growing. "But poor Steven doesn't."

"I'll explain when he comes back." He ran his hands through his hair and then rubbed his eyes. "Damn, I'm tired. I hope I make it through more than one show."

3

Promoted & Dead

"Don't you dare leave this room, Heather Robbins!" Phyllis was lounging in bed, her eye mask resting on her forehead.

"I'm not waiting for you to transform yourself from evil witch to evil witch with a full face of makeup before I eat breakfast. The corporate retreat won't crumble if we don't eat together." Heather was nearly shaking with anger.

"I'm your boss," Phyllis snarled as she sat up in bed. The implications were clear.

"Go to Hell, you old bat!" Heather screamed, rushing away from the room. At that point, she didn't care if she lost her job. Spending the last eight hours with the bitching, snoring beast had been more than enough.

"I'm just gonna leave too," came a meek voice from the doorway of the bathroom. The newest nurse at the hospital, Maliayah, had also shared a room with the feuding women. "I'll save you a seat at the table."

* * *

"Where have you been?" Maliyah asked when Heather joined her at the table. She was almost halfway through her meal.

"I took a walk around the grounds to cool off. I figured it wouldn't be wise to throw cereal in her face at this point." Both women laughed.

"What is it between you two, anyway?" the new nurse asked.

Heather launched into the story of her mother's history with Nurse Ratched. Just as she finished by punctuating the story with her empty coffee cup slammed on the table, the whole building seemed to shake. No one was sure in which order the other series of sounds and events happened, but there was a shattering of glass, a scream from inside the dining room, and a loud thud.

The entire room came to a standstill, and those who had been facing the large double-paned dining room windows rushed over to look out. Maliyah just stared with her mouth open and pointed.

"What is it, what's wrong?" Heather asked the woman across from her.

"Someone just fell from the sky."

"You go see if they need medical help," Heather delegated. "I'll be right behind you while I call 911."

* * *

Something was slowly waking Loralin, and she wanted no part of it. She was almost positive that sleep wasn't done with her yet. It had to still be dark outside.

"Loralin. The Phone. Answer it," Devin's sleepy voice murmured from beside her.

The sound of his voice from her bed wasn't anything new. They often fell asleep watching TV together. But something felt off. Maybe it had been the fact that someone was calling her during the night. She popped one eye open and noticed it was, in fact, daytime, and when her eye focused on the clock on her bedside table, she noticed she had slept in for almost an hour. When her phone began to ring again, she groaned. The morning was there, like it or not. "Hello, this is Loralin."

"Hey, boss, it's Maureen. There's been another murder."

Loralin dropped the phone, then picked it back up and mumbled a goodbye.

"Loralin?" Devin's voice was distressed.

"I know," she whispered. "I can't believe there's been another murder."

"Oh God," he groaned. "That's terrible, but that's not what I'm talking about. Look down."

Loralin did as Devin told her to, and she gasped. How and why was she naked? As if they were acting on their own, her hands grasped the blanket and pulled it over her breasts.

"Loralin did we..."

She turned her head to look over her shoulder at him. He was shirtless, and there was no hint of his pajama bottoms above the blanket covering his lap. "I... She shook her head. "Yeah, I'm pretty sure we did."

"Yeah," he sighed in agreement as he picked up the empty wine bottle on the night table and set it back down. "I remember now. And we weren't even that drunk."

The sound of sirens cut straight through their fog of remembrance. "We'll talk about this later," Loralin stated matter-of-factly. Right now, we have to get to the inn. I hung up on Maureen before she could tell me who was dead this time."

***

All of the activity seemed to be happening behind the Inn. Loralin and Devin followed two uniformed Elk River police officers around the back and stopped at the edge of the gathered crowd. Phyllis Palmer lay dead as they came on the ground outside the dining room. For the first time ever, she was silent.

"Is Loralin here yet?" Miles's voice came from above. When they looked up, he was standing in a broken window frame. "There you are. Meet me at the front desk, please."

Loralin and Devin moved away from the crowd and walked along the side of the building to the side steps and onto the porch. They were both quiet. They had two very contradictory things on their mind. "What do you need me for, Miles?" she asked with an exasperated sigh.

"Is…is everything okay? You're usually the first to want to become involved in things like this." Her ex-husband looked worried.

"Sorry," she said. "I just have stuff on my mind. Do we know what happened yet?" She put her personal thoughts at the back of her mind and thought of Phyllis lying dead on the grounds of her property.

"Well, of course, we won't know officially until the initial investigation and autopsy are complete, but it looks like someone choked Phyllis and then tossed her out the window."

"Damn," Devin said. "I knew she wasn't well-liked by some, but…"

"Phyllis Palmer was hated by everyone, my friend," Miles said. "And that's what is going to make solving her murder so hard. That and the fact that the forensics guys are not going to be able to make it until tomorrow."

Loralin felt tears escaping down her face. "We're being closed down again. The inn will never survive this time."

Devin's arm wrapped around his… what was she now that they had slept together? He was going to stick with 'best friend'. It was easiest. He didn't have to think too deeply about that one. "It'll be okay. Miles, you can use the office to interview people. Loralin and I will help in any way we can."

Miles nodded and took Loralin's arm in his hand. "I guess I'll start with you."

"Why?" she asked. "Because I probably hated her more than anyone?"

"I wouldn't say that right now, my dear," Miles returned with a chuckle. "But no, I chose you first because it's your inn and you are right here with me already. Devin will be next."

As Loralin let herself be led away, her eyes caught Devin's. They both realized that their alibi was each other. And they'd been doing something they didn't want to talk about yet, especially to her ex-husband.

* * *

"Okay, I guess we will start with the basics," Miles said as he sat down behind Loralin's desk with his notepad and pen. "Where were you this morning between six and seven a.m.?"

"I was in bed."

"Do you have anyone who can vouch for you?"

"Yes. Devin. He was there with me."

Miles's eyebrow raised. "He…" he cleared his throat, "He

was in bed with you?"

"Yes," Loralin admitted. "We fell asleep watching TV."

"And he knows for sure you were there?"

"Well, yeah," she said with a sigh. "The phone woke us up at about seven thirty with the news. I told Devin, and then we got our clothes on and hurried over here."

Miles stared at his ex-wife with his mouth open. "Got your clothes on? Aren't those the clothes you were wearing yesterday?"

Loralin blushed. "We changed from our night clothes into what we wore yesterday just to speed things up," she stammered.

"You do remember that I was married to you for over twenty years. I know what that blush means. Did you sleep with Devin?"

Loralin stood up and glared at her ex. "That would be none of your business! It happened before the murder timeline."

"Happened or would have happened," Miles said with a hearty laugh.

"You know," Loralin grumped. "It's times like this when I remember why I divorced you."

"Alright, alright," he said as his laughter died out and his voice became serious. "I won't tell anyone that you're more than friends. Although you had me going for years."

"We are just friends!!!" she cried. "Last night... last night... I don't know what happened. It just..."

"So," Miles said, trying to decide if he believed her. "You're saying that last night just happened, and it's the only time it's happened?"

"Yes!" she exclaimed. "We haven't even had a chance to talk about it yet. Please, can we just drop it?"

Miles closed his notebook and smirked. "Yeah. I'll pretend I never heard it. After I talk to Devin, of course. Can you send him in and go round up the next witness?"

"Sure," Loralin said, hoping she could trust her ex with this secret. "Who is after Devin?"

"Our Daughter."

Loralin suddenly remembered her daughter's words from the night before about killing the now-dead head nurse. The knot in the pit of her stomach that had been there since Maureen's call doubled in size.

4

Friends & Lovers

Loralin and Devin sat at the table in the inn's dining room with Miles. They were eating a quick dinner to discuss the day's happenings.

"Do you have any prime suspects yet?" Devin asked.

"Anyone here who had ever met Phyllis Palmer?" Miles sighed, rubbing his forehead. "I'm beginning to believe that this case may never be solved."

Loralin chuckled. "Either that or you'll have to lock up the whole town of Elk River and half of Casper."

The big, strong police detective, more from width than height, let a whimper of a laugh escape before he sat up straight and cleared his throat. "I know what you two are thinking," he murmured. "But you are not to become involved in this case in any way. I really mean it this time. Stay out of it!"

Devin and Loralin looked at each other and smiled, thinking about how they had solved the other murder that had taken place there. "Well, if you solve it, then we won't have to get involved now, will we?" Loralin said. "And solve it quickly. Please. This inn can't take much more murder and mayhem.

Miles grunted and started eating his dinner, but he didn't say anything else until the food was gone and he was standing to leave. "I guess I'd better get down to the station and bring the chief up to speed on everything. I can't believe how much I miss having Jackie as my partner. It's all been downhill since she moved to Sheridan. And Chief Morris is too by the book. I don't think he's had an original idea in twenty years."

Miles didn't even wait for goodbyes before heading out of the dining room. "I was hoping the Chief would extend his leave of absence," Loralin said with a sigh. The insufferable man was sure to make this murder harder to solve than the last one.

"He's that bad, huh?" Devin asked.

"Yes," Loralin said, a triumphant look in her eyes. "Miles is going to need our help."

"I was afraid you'd say that," Devin groaned. "I can't help but think we should stay out of this one. It's bound to get too personal."

"Personal?" Loralin questioned. "What do you mean?"

Devin's gaze never left his hands as they lay entwined on the table. "I heard two of the deputies talking. I guess bets are being taken on whether your daughter or Chef Pierre will be arrested first."

"Oh, for fuck's sake," Loralin ground out. "That's all the more reason to help Miles."

Devin knew she was probably right, but he didn't look forward to defying Miles. "I know, but where do we start this time?"

"I haven't quite figured that out yet."

* * *

Shortly after dinner, the two walked down the path leading to the home they shared. Neither one wanted to bring up the subject that stood between them. In the end, Loralin was the one who couldn't take the silence anymore. "So, about last night... I'm not sure what to say."

"I know," Devin agreed. He almost looked relieved that he hadn't had to bring it up. "I'm sorry, Loralin. I didn't mean for it to happen. I was tired and had some wine..."

Loralin opened the front door of the three-bedroom cottage that had once belonged to her grandparents. "So... it sounds like you regret it, like you wish it had never happened."

"What? No, I..." Devin's words were interrupted by loud, happy voices coming from the kitchen.

"Mom, Devin! Come in here and join us."

"Hanna?" Loralin squealed. "What are you doing here?" Her oldest daughter lived halfway across the state in Evanston. How had they made it through the flood? Local roads were pretty much reopened, but the freeway wouldn't reopen until late morning.

"Matthew's boss flew him in to check on their fields, and I tagged along," she said, taking her husband's hand.

"Oh, baby, it's so good to have you here. Loralin hugged both of her daughters and then her son-in-law. "Did your sister tell you what happened to Phyllis?"

"Yeah, she did." Hanna's voice was now soft and mournful. "And tomorrow Matthew is going back to Casper to fly out for a business trip, and I'm going to stay here until this whole mess is over."

Loralin's face lit up like it was Christmas, and then she brought on her teasing smile. "Well, knowing how slow your father and Chief Morris are, that means you might be here until the beginning of the twenty-second century."

Everyone in the room laughed. "Shall we move this to the lounge?" Devin asked. "I, for one, have been standing all day."

As much as Loralin wanted to finish her conversation with him, she knew he was right. It was important to spend time with her family. It would do her a world of good.

* * *

Hanna and Matthew were settled in the guest room, and Heather was put in Devin's room, leaving him and Loralin sharing her room. It's not like they hadn't done it before, so she was sure they could do it again. And they'd be able to discuss what had happened the night before.

While Devin was locking up and getting her a glass of water, Loralin decided to get changed. All she could think of was curling up under the covers and talking to him about the sudden change their relationship had taken.

"Damn," she heard softly from behind her, followed by a thump and a light splash.

She slowly turned her head to see that the bathroom door had crept fully open on its own as it had often lately. The entire back of her body was on display, red lace underwear and all. The front was featured in the mirror in front of her. Devin could view it all. "I guess I should get that door fixed."

"I... umm..." He stammered. "Yeah."

"Oh, come on, Devin. It's not like you didn't see all this last night." She turned fully away from the mirror to face him. She wasn't usually this brave, but for some reason, his shock bothered her, and she felt the need to face it head-on.

"Well, actually," he said, his expression changing from one of shock to a smile of pleasure. "To be honest, I don't remember exactly what I saw last night. We were all over each other and not really looking. Just feeling and tasting, umm, mostly."

Loralin felt a bit self-conscious all of a sudden, but only for one brief moment. "Well then," she whispered. "What do you think?"

"I think you're the most beautiful woman I've ever seen." There was no hesitation in his words, and she believed every single one.

"Wow. I don't know what to say to that." Her whole body flushed, and Devin's smile grew mischievous.

"Maybe now isn't the time for words. It's only eight o'clock, and I remember a bit about last night being pretty damn incredible. I think maybe we should refresh our memories."

Loralin was now looking deep into Devin's eyes as he reached out to caress her face. "How did you get over here so fast?"

Devin never did answer; he just kissed her, moving from her mouth to her jaw and back again.

* * *

"Oh my God! That was incredible!" Loralin said between gasps.

"Even more incredible than last night," Devin agreed. "How did we ever wait so long to do that?"

"I don't know. But I could do that every day if I had to." She was smiling at him, and he was smiling right back at her.

When Devin's phone went off from the bedside table, he dragged his eyes from her beautiful mouth. What he saw on the screen stole his smile and the light in his eyes.

"Who was it?" Loralin asked when he didn't answer the call.

"My mother." He went to the bathroom and locked the door tight.

In that moment, she knew she'd lost him. And her heart started to hurt. When he came back, he was dressed in PJ bottoms and a t-shirt he'd left in her bathroom the night before. "I don't think what we did was right. It's best if it doesn't happen again." He grabbed a pillow and blanket from the closet and moved out to the couch.

Loralin got out of bed and dressed before closing the bedroom door. Was it bad that she'd almost hoped that this was the beginning of something special? But he was probably right. They were better off the way they were before. No one heard her as she cried herself to sleep.

5

Mama Bear Awakens

Loralin was in a state somewhere between wakefulness and light sleep when she felt the bed dip beside her. A warm, strong arm snaked around her stomach and pulled her close.

"I'm so sorry. I'm just confused, and things are so complicated." Devin's voice was quiet but desperate.

"You don't think I feel the same way?" Loralin asked. "I don't think this is something that can be turned on and off. Our bond is so strong, but not unbreakable. We can't play games with it."

"I know, but…" He hesitated for only a moment. "This is exactly what my mum accused us of, and we always insisted it could never happen."

Loralin rolled over so she was facing him. "And now we have to figure out exactly why it happened and if it's right or wrong."

"Yeah," he whispered. "And, why it's about to happen again." His lips brushed against hers, and she didn't resist. Neither of them stopped to think. They just felt whatever came over them and hoped they could figure it out eventually. Their bond depended on it.

For the second morning in a row, Loralin and Devin were woken by the ringing of her phone. They had overslept again. "This is Loralin."

"Hey, it's Maureen. The state forensics guys are here. Will you be here soon?"

"Shit. I almost forgot my inn was the scene of yet another murder. We'll be right there."

Devin was already up and in the bathroom when she hung up the phone. She heard the shower start and rushed to join him. "Hey," he said with a smile as she opened the shower door and slid in.

"Hey. I figure this will save time and water."

Devin chuckled. "I never figured you for the type who wanted to save the planet."

Loralin chuckled with him. "Oh yeah. I'm as green as they come." She knew they should hurry, but they took turns washing each other, then finally, reluctantly turned the water off. "I guess we'll figure us out later and take care of the problems at the inn now, huh?"

"Probably a good idea," Devin agreed. "We have our whole lives to figure us out, but we need to get Phyllis's murder solved ASAP."

Loralin was pretty sure she knew why her heart did a little flip-flop. It was the words 'our whole lives'. Was it possible? Did she even want that?

* * *

All hell was breaking loose when Loralin and Devin arrived at the inn. But that was nothing new. It seemed to happen a lot since the grand opening.

Forensic techs were everywhere, the phones were ringing off the hook, and Miles was walking with Heather out of the dining room. Two patrol officers were following them.

Loralin rushed over, her eyes trying to read Miles's demeanor. Something was wrong. "What's going on?"

"Daddy's arresting me for Phyllis's murder," Heather said, her voice shaky. "I didn't do it, Mama."

"Of course, you didn't," Loralin reassured her daughter. "What the hell is going on, Miles?"

"Morris wants an arrest, and because Heather was heard wishing Phyllis harm on more than one occasion and has no verifiable alibi, he wants her arrested," Miles said, not meeting his ex's gaze. "He's not happy about two murders in a row in our small town. He wants to send a message."

"That's ridiculous!" Loralin snarled. "There's no actual proof! Hell, forensics isn't even collected yet."

"I know," Miles said quietly, through gritted teeth, so as not to create a scene like his ex-wife was doing. "But I have to do my job, and right now, that is taking Heather in."

"Yeah," Loralin returned loud enough for everyone to hear. "Well, maybe it's time for you and Morris to find new jobs!"

"Mama, don't," Heather cut in. "I'll be okay. Just try to get me out as fast as you can, please."

Loralin stormed off, but not before she heard Miles say, "Heather Robbins, you're under arrest for the murder of Phyllis Palmer." At least he had the good grace to sound like it was killing him to say them.

* * *

Loralin knew it would take a while for her daughter to be processed, so she set about her daily routine at the inn. While Devin notified future guests of the temporary closure and offered them help in either rebooking or finding other accommodations, she sat in her office contacting suppliers about replenishing the supplies she'd used when they were the temporary flood shelter. The city and county would reimburse her, but there was no telling when that would actually happen. She had just hung up the phone when there was a knock on her office door. "Enter."

A young forensics tech poked her head in. "Mrs. Robbins, my boss would like a word with you. He's in the room where the incident occurred."

"Okay. I need just a minute. Tell him I'll be right there." She wanted to get Devin to go with her. The man who led the forensics team was a dream, one she didn't want to complicate her life with. He would act as a buffer. Especially if he was now more than what he'd once been. She couldn't think like that yet, though. Their three 'episodes' together had most likely been born from sadness and anger caused by the flood and the murder.

* * *

"I wonder what he wants?" Devin questioned as they made their way up to the third-floor room.

"Who knows," she said as her mind continued to wander to

places it shouldn't be.

The young officer who'd come to fetch her was waiting outside the room and escorted them in. The man she was there to see had his back to them.

"Boss. Mrs. Robbins is here."

He turned, and a smile lit his face. "It's good to see you again, Mrs. Robbins. I just wish the circumstances were better this time."

"You and me both," she said, her expression purposely blank. "Is there something you need from me?"

"I just wanted to let you know that we are taking the entire casing of the window to test for pressure cracks, rot, and breakage. You should be able to have your contractor come in after we leave to board it up."

Loralin was listening, but her eyes were taking in everything about the window that Phyllis was thrown through. She now knew why they were taking what remained of the window, and she also knew how she was going to get her daughter off the hook. "Can I take a few pictures before you dismantle it?"

"Umm…" the man looked at her warily. "I… yeah, I guess so. Just don't touch anything or go past this line, please."

Once a few pictures were snapped, Loralin and Devin left and headed back downstairs. "So," Devin asked. "What was that all about?"

Loralin had a shit-eating grin on her face that she got quite often when she was solving a mystery. "If the autopsy report comes back like I think it will, I'm about to prove that Morris is a douche, and I'm going to get my baby out of jail."

"Okay…" Devin hesitated. "But Miles told you to stay out of it."

Loralin laughed. "He told us to stay out of it, not just me.

But if he wants to save his daughter and get this case solved, he's going to have to let us help."

"I really don't like the sound of that," Devin groaned. "Please tell me we're not going to steal files from the police station again."

Loralin huffed. "We didn't steal them. We photocopied them."

And just like that, as he had feared, the old lady who solved crimes with her hapless sidekick was back. One day, he was going to end up in jail because of her. He hoped that this was not that day.

* * *

Devin drove the car he'd recently bought toward Elk River's police headquarters. "Why did you insist we take my car?"

"It's a sports model. It's faster than my SUV." Loralin looked out the window as the scenery of central Wyoming flashed by. "Park in front of the building if you can. It will give us a quicker getaway if needed."

"Oh God," he groaned. "After we park, I'm giving you the keys. I'm not losing my new license because of this."

"That's fine," Loralin murmured. "I'm sure Miles will help willingly, but if he doesn't…"

Devin pulled up to the curb and stopped. "I hope you have a plan."

"I do," she said, finally smiling again. "Let's get this over with."

It wasn't until they reached the door of the precinct that they realized they'd held hands the whole way. They looked at each other and then separated before heading inside.

The woman sitting at the watch desk was someone Loralin didn't recognize. "Hello, I'm here to see Detective Robbins."

"I'm sorry. I believe he's working on a case right now."

Loralin sighed. She hated breaking in the new people. "He'll see me. I'm Loralin Robbins, his ex-wife. He arrested our daughter this morning."

The uniformed woman, whose name tag said L. Henderson, drew in a quick breath. "Just a moment." She picked up the phone and dialed. A minute later, Miles came out of his office and motioned them over.

"They've already taken Heather to Boone," he said, looking like he was waiting to be clobbered by his ex.

"Can we go sit in your office and talk?" Loralin asked.

Miles turned and looked at his office, then back to Loralin. "I'm not so sure that's a good idea after the last case."

"Come on, Miles," Devin said in a voice that invoked the feel of a man-to-man conversation. "She's not going to copy your files this time. I promise I won't let her."

Miles stood, looking back and forth between the two. "I guess it's alright," he finally gave in. "Everything is kept on tablets and computers now anyway. Except for my notes, of course. But I have those hidden. "He led the way back to the office. Once they were settled in their seats, he motioned for Loralin to tell him why she was there.

"I want you to let us in on the investigation." Before she could say any more, Miles had his answer.

"Absolutely Not!"

"Just listen to her, man," Devin said a bit more harshly than he'd planned.

"Go ahead, Loralin," Miles agreed. "But my answer will be

the same."

Loralin rolled her eyes and then winked at Devin. "You have to let us help you, Miles. You have no one else since Jackie transferred."

"Captain Morris," he said, but immediately regretted it.

"He's not going to help you," she insisted. "He's more worried about how the department looks, so he can keep his job. Plus, he was the worst detective this department has ever seen."

"I can keep him under control and away from the investigation," Miles seethed. He hated being one-upped by anyone, let alone his ex-wife.

"Like you did this morning?" she shot back. "When he forced you to arrest your innocent daughter."

Miles's face turned red, and for a moment, he looked like he was about to explode. Devin and Loralin watched patiently as his breathing and coloring returned to normal. "Please, Miles, let us help. We're all you've got." Devin couldn't believe those words had come out of his mouth.

"I already know how to free Heather; you might as well let us help with the rest."

"Fine," he grumbled. "How on earth can you free our daughter? Morris is determined to make an example out of her."

"Once I get the preliminary autopsy report, I can prove she didn't kill Phyllis. Or at least create reasonable doubt until forensics is back." Loralin was back in sleuth mode, and she probably wouldn't leave it until the case was solved.

"Damn it," Miles groaned as his fist came down on his desk. "Morris wants the findings kept quiet for now. If I tell you, I'll lose my job."

"I saw them on the watch commander's desk," Devin said.

"You create a distraction, and we'll take care of the rest."

Miles looked at Devin, his eyes narrowed. "Do you really enjoy doing this? You can tell her no."

Devin shrugged. "Sometimes, when the adrenaline gets pumping, it's kinda fun... I guess."

"Yep!" Miles said with a chuckle. "You're in love with her. That's the only thing that explains it. Your tryst the other night was no accident. It was a natural progression." They didn't think he'd ever stop chuckling and shaking his head.

"Wow," Loralin whispered. She was afraid to look at Devin and see his reaction, but she did anyway. He looked like a deer caught in the headlights.

"Okay then," Miles said as his laughter stopped and he stood. "Let's get this over with. I'll distract Linda, and you get the info you need and free our girl."

* * *

Loralin had the information she needed, so she motioned for Miles to stop talking to Sargent Henderson and join them.

"So, what's the plan now?" he asked.

Loralin looked very satisfied with herself as she turned to her ex. "You need to get me in to see Morris."

Miles slumped. "I'm going to have to get a new job, aren't I?"

Both Devin and Loralin laughed. "Nope," they said in unison.

"Take us to him," Loralin ordered. "And no matter what happens, stay quiet."

Reluctantly, Miles did as she asked. Two knocks on the chief's door, and they were inside.

"What can I do for you, Mrs. Robbins?" He seemed bothered

by the intrusion.

"I want my daughter freed and home from Boone by tonight." She figured it was best to start with the direct approach and leave the threats and surprises for later if needed.

"Might I remind you that your daughter looks very guilty, Mrs. Robbins? She will remain incarcerated until the investigation proves that guilt."

"Might I remind you, Chief," Loralin ground out. "That the forensics weren't even done being collected when you had your henchman make that arrest." She paused, praying that Miles would remain quiet, and he did. "I want my daughter released tonight."

"Mrs Robbins," he said politely, trying another approach. "We need to wrap this up quickly, and at this point, all fingers point to your daughter. I'm truly sorry, but that's the way it is."

His 'kind' smile made Loralin sick to her stomach. "According to the autopsy report, Phyllis was already dead when she was thrown out the window. My daughter is five feet nothing and 100 pounds. Ms. Palmer was six feet and 200 pounds. There is no way my daughter could have lifted and thrown that woman's dead weight out the window! And forensics took half the side of my building with them to prove that. I suggest you set her free now, or I will have to give one hell of a story to the press locally and in Casper."

Chief Morris looked like he had been slapped. "Well, that autopsy information was confidential. It looks like we might be looking for a new detective here soon." His look turned menacing, and his gaze moved to Miles.

Loralin felt bad that she put her ex-husband through all this, but it was almost over, and they would have their daughter home. "Oh, Miles didn't tell me. But you really should tell whoever opens the reports not to leave them sitting on the Watch Commander's desk for the world to see."

Chief Morris looked like he was about to lose his mind and tear the room apart, but all he did was pull a form out of his drawer and start filling it out. With a flourish, he signed it and handed it to Miles. "Your daughter will be brought to the inn by nightfall. Now get the hell out of my office!"

6

Exchange Of Information

Loralin and Devin sat on one of the overstuffed couches that were scattered around the inn's grand entrance. They were waiting for Heather's arrival. They'd been entrusted to bring her to her father's house, where his wife, Meredith, a caterer, would put on a feast for the entire family. Hanna was already there.

"So help me, if they mistreated her…" Loralin seethed.

"Hey, calm down," Devin reassured her. "I'm sure she's fine." His arm rested on her shoulders.

"She better be, or there is going to be hell to pay for Chief Arnold Morris."

Devin caressed her shoulder. "Don't let anyone hear you say that."

Loralin just grunted and continued to look out the window. "There she is!"

A Campbell County corrections vehicle pulled up outside the inn, and Heather stepped out. She said something to the driver and then headed inside.

"Oh, baby!" Loralin sang out. "Are you okay?"

"I'm fine, Mama," she said with a laugh. "I never even saw the inside of a cell."

"Really?" Devin asked his friend, whom he had met well before he and Loralin started talking.

"Yep." Heather hugged her mother tightly. "Daddy told them what was going on, and they let me hang out in the director's office and watch TV and play on my phone. I would have slept on the couch if you hadn't gotten me sprung when you did."

Loralin released her daughter. "I'm so glad. Now, why don't you go to my office and freshen up? We'll head to your dad's for dinner after."

Once Heather was out of earshot, Devin turned to Loralin. "What's on your mind?"

"I… I'm not sure. It's almost like Miles knew that I was going to put the pieces together. But why didn't he just go to Morris with it himself?"

"Who knows with Miles?" Devin sighed, rolling his eyes. "Sometimes I swear he's a genius in disguise, and other times, I think he's the second-worst detective the Elk River PD has ever seen."

* * *

The drive to Miles's house only took ten minutes. Hanna was already there helping Meredith prepare dinner. Once the family was settled together in the living room for drinks, Loralin pulled her ex into his home office. "Did you already know the stuff I used against Morris?"

Miles moved back and rested his butt on the edge of his desk. "Yes."

When he wasn't more forthcoming, Loralin pressed on. "Then why in the hell didn't you go to Morris with it?!"

"I knew he wouldn't listen to me, and he might even try to fire me for insubordination, so I figured I'd let you do it."

Loralin gave him a harsh look. "Damn it, Miles, what if I'd never put two and two together?"

He laughed, looking so proud of himself. "Who do you think told your hottie forensics boss to make sure he kept you in the loop about the window?"

"Still Miles," she said, her anger dying down. "Next time, just tell me. I might not have connected the dots, and our daughter could have been in jail for God knows how long!"

"Well," he returned. "This way, I could honestly deny any knowledge. But okay, I get what you're saying. I'll be more forthcoming in the future."

Somehow, she felt like he was being condescending, but that wasn't like him. With a nod, she pulled a tablet out of her bag. "You're still planning on sharing your files with me, right?"

With a sigh, he stood up straight and reached for the tablet. "You head back out to the others, and I'll do the dirty work. That way, you can honestly say that you never saw it happen."

By the time he came out of his office, her tablet in hand with almost one gig of new info on it, dinner was being served.

* * *

Dinner went by with only a smattering of random conversations. Everyone was playing catch-up with Hanna and getting to know Devin even more. But by the time dessert was served, the conversation had turned toward the murder.

"I can't say as I'm surprised it happened," Hanna said. "I personally don't know of anyone so hated. I'll never forget the day Heather told me she would be working with her. I was so glad I had decided not to become a nurse."

Everyone at the table chuckled. Loralin looked at Heather and smiled. "I bet today you were wishing you had taken that job in Boone instead."

"I've been wishing that for a while now, Mama." Heather smiled back at her mother and then turned to Miles. "Daddy, who do you think could have done it?"

Miles reached over and squeezed his daughter's hand. "I just don't know. Anyone could have had a motive. Those who knew her didn't like her. Chef Pierre hated her from the time they were married. Hell, I'm sure there were even patients she must have pissed off. We're going to start by looking at everyone who was at the inn, though; those who knew her and those who were stranded because of the flood."

"Well, I'd offer to get you a list of people she pissed off at the hospital," Heather offered but they've put me on leave until this whole mess is straightened out."

"They aren't going to fire you, are they?" Devin asked. "I mean, that would be completely unfair since you're innocent."

"I've been guaranteed my job back," she informed all those at the table who looked at her with interest. "I'm thinking it might be time for a change, though."

The group went silent, and Meredith took the opportunity to clear the table. Once again, even in death, Phyllis had brought a room to its knees.

* * *

Devin and Loralin were prepared to leave once they'd visited with the family for an hour. "Who's coming with us?"

"I am!" Hanna said as she stood up.

"I'll stay here so Devin can have his room back," Heather said with a yawn. "Besides, I don't think I could move further than the guest room if I tried."

Loralin hugged her oldest daughter. "Get some rest. You can come out to the inn tomorrow, and we can spend some time together if you want. We reopen at noon, but that's not a big deal. I should have plenty of time."

"Yeah, and if mom is busy, you can spend time with me," Hanna interjected. "Goodnight, everyone."

On the drive home, Devin and Loralin stayed quiet. They both seriously wanted to talk about the case, but with Hanna in the car, they figured it would be best to wait. They had their own way of doing things and didn't want to involve the young woman in any way.

"So, are you two going to hide out in your bedroom?" Hanna asked as they pulled into the driveway. The tone of voice she used didn't go unnoticed by either of them.

"We might discuss the case," Devin finally said.

"We all know there is more going on than sleuthing," Hanna said with a laugh.

"Please don't," Loralin insisted. "We had some… some things come up that could have changed that, but we are dealing with it. I'm sure my nosy family will be the first to know if anything changes permanently."

Hanna knew better than to say anything else, so she left the car and headed straight to the guest room.

"Was it that obvious?" Loralin asked, afraid to look at Devin.

"Well, you got kinda loud the other night," he teased. And

yeah, knowing us, it probably shows all over our faces."

With a sigh, Loralin got out of the car. "You grab snacks and drinks, and I'll meet you at the dining room table with my tablet. We need to solve this damn case."

* * *

Both of us using this tablet is going to be a pain in the ass," Devin commented as he put a snack tray and two sodas on the table. "I like being able to spread the pictures out to look at all at once."

"Me too," Loralin echoed. "That's why I brought the printer from my office home while you were leading the staff meeting this afternoon. It's on my dresser."

"Genius!" Devin didn't miss a beat, skirting around the table to go grab the printer.

Loralin busied herself hooking the device up while Devin took his first peek at the files on the tablet. By the time they sat down together, with paper copies of files and pictures spread out between them, it was nearly nine o'clock.

"They really don't have much to go on yet." Devin shuffled through the crime scene photos until they were pretty much ingrained in his brain. "I just don't see anything out of place."

"I know," Loralin said with a yawn. "I guess there's not much to do until the initial forensics reports come in. For all we know, the killer was stupid and left their fingerprints all over everything, and we'll know who the killer is by tomorrow."

"Yeah," he mumbled even though his mind was a million miles away. "Shouldn't we have the fingerprint results by now, though? Miles's men did them two days ago."

Loralin was gathering all of the papers off the table and organizing them in a folder. "No, Morris made Miles send them all to the lab in Cheyenne and requested that they all be processed at the same time as the other evidence."

"Of course he did," Devin growled. "I really don't like that man. Do you think Miles will be able to get a subpoena for hospital records about Nurse Ratched?"

Before Loralin could answer, her cell phone rang. "It's Heather. Hey, baby, what's up?"

"Hey, Mom, sorry to call so late, but Dad and I wanted to let you know that he called Judge Porter and got the subpoena to get Phyllis's records from both of the hospitals she's worked at."

"Oh, that's great! I'm surprised Judge Porter agreed to do it." The old man was a stickler for truth and justice and rarely gave out warrants and such unless there were twenty kinds of proof that it was one hundred percent needed.

"It helps that I dated his son until he came out as gay. The Porters love me."

"I guess that makes sense," Loralin commented. "I just hope that now we can make a proper suspect list. I don't feel like it was someone local."

"I hope so, too, Mama. I'll bring you copies of the files tomorrow. Goodnight."

Loralin hung up the phone and brought Devin up to speed. "You up for a movie or our show tonight?"

"Nah," he said with a yawn. "I think I'm just going to head to bed." Kissing her forehead, he disappeared down the hall to his own room.

"We can't avoid this forever," she whispered to herself. It was going to be another sleepless night. This time it wouldn't be because of a crazy night of passion. It would be because she wouldn't be able to stop wondering what the hell had happened between them.

7

Sabotage?

Loralin woke up at six am and headed to the inn alone. The place had to be ready to reopen by noon, and she wasn't the type who liked to leave all the details to her staff. She liked to be hands-on as much as possible.

The days were getting warmer, and it would soon be time for the summer rush. Elk River had its fair share of tourists. Despite the bumbling of the local police department, Elk River had a lot to offer. Some of the most beautiful scenery Wyoming had was less than half an hour away. And the town's namesake was not only gorgeous territory, but it also offered some of the best fishing in the state. And when people got tired of nature and down-home cafe cooking, Casper was only thirty minutes away.

"Good morning, Loralin," Maureen said with a smile.

She looked up at the young desk clerk, who would soon become the assistant manager, and returned her greeting. She didn't even realize that she'd already arrived at the inn. She completely blanked out everything but what was plaguing her mind at the moment.

A few people milled around the lobby, but everything else was quiet. The last of their flood-related guests would be heading out, so things would be completely back to normal. "Maureen, how many guests are we expecting today?"

The young woman hit a few keys on her keyboard. "Well, we have eight rooms still occupied after the flood victims leave. No one is checking out, and twelve rooms are filling up by tonight. By the end of the week, we should almost have a packed house."

Loralin couldn't help but let out a muffled squeal. "So, we didn't lose anyone because of the murder?"

"We didn't," Maureen chuckled. "But I think a lot of people thought it was a tragic accident."

Loralin knew that the desk clerk was probably right. But at this point, she was happy with anything as long as it kept the inn running. Her biggest fear was that two murders would be too much for her dream to handle.

A grumpy fake Frenchman's loud, angry voice wafting in from the kitchen switched her focus, and she hurried to see what was upsetting the chef so much. Loralin was almost run over by their newest employee as he fled the kitchen to the chorus of crashing pots and pans.

"Poor excuse of a waiter," the chef hollered directly at Loralin. "I don't want him in my kitchen anymore!"

"I… I thought Jeremy was a housekeeper," Loralin stammered. The young man who'd nearly trampled her had been hired by Devin just five days before, as a housekeeper, not a waiter.

"He was traumatized by the bitch's murder; I liked the kid. I felt bad for him and offered to try him out in the kitchen. He almost ruined everything!" The man was beet red, and his wild hand gestures had almost clobbered several of his staff.

Loralin looked around the room. Everything seemed to be running smoothly, and the only thing out of place was the pot rack that he'd obviously felled himself during his fit of rage. She had never met someone so particular about his workplace. "I'll go talk to him," was the only thing she could think to say as she too fled the kitchen.

Jeremy Orville was sitting in the employee lounge with his head in his hands. "Hey," Loralin said calmly as she sat across from him. "Just ignore Chef. He's mostly hot air."

The young man looked up at her and smiled. "Thanks. I sure made a mess of things."

She studied him for a moment. "Are you too disturbed by what happened to work in housekeeping?"

"What? No! I was just kinda freaked out. I'm okay now. Chef Pierre just really seemed nice and like he could use the extra help, so…" He shrugged and slumped in his seat again.

"Well then, clock out from your ill-fated kitchen shift and come back in for your scheduled housekeeping shift. I don't see why we can't just forget about what happened and start fresh."

The young man couldn't have been over twenty, although he didn't look much over eighteen. "Thank you so much, Ma'am! I'll be back for my shift tomorrow." He stood quickly and was gone.

Loralin made a note to talk to Chef Pierre about hiring kitchen staff out from under the hotel, and then she headed to her office, hoping that Devin would be there.

* * *

"You okay, Dev?" Loralin took a seat behind her desk and looked at her hotel manager. He was sitting across from her with a blank expression covering his face.

"Yeah," he sighed. "The break Lisa Marie and I were on is over. She said she wants to stay single."

Loralin battled between elation, guilt, and sadness for Devin. On one hand, she was sad because the two had seemed to get along so well. However, she was also kind of happy because she liked having him to herself, no matter what their feelings were for each other, and no matter whether they were admitted or denied. But that's when the guilt butted in. "What happened?"

"She said the age difference was starting to get to her, and she told me that I probably shouldn't date anyone else until I got a handle on my feelings for you."

"Oh." Loralin wasn't quite sure what to say. A lot of people hadn't been able to handle her friendship with Devin. She'd thought for sure Lisa Marie was different.

"Yeah. I tried to tell her that we were just friends. I tried to explain to her about the bond we have, but…" He shrugged and picked at an imaginary blemish on his slacks.

"But are we just friends? I mean, even I don't know what we are anymore."

"I know. I just, I'm not sure what I'm feeling and what you're feeling and what we should do about what happened. But hell, I missed you last night. Every time I leave your side, I want to kiss you goodbye. But it also terrifies me. Our age gap, expectations from my mother, and the question of can friends who've had sex still be just friends? It's all so confusing, and I just don't have the capacity to work through it right now. I mean, with the murder, and this thing with us, my so-called relationship with Lisa Marie, my mother, my father, and brother…" Once he realized he was babbling, he stopped talking and looked at Loralin.

"Well, I'm pretty confused too," she admitted. "Maybe we should just go about our days and deal with our issues and outside problems, and whatever happens with us happens. Eventually, we'll be able to deal with it, right?"

"Yeah," he said, cheering up. "Nobody says everything has to have a label. We can worry about that once our stress level is down a bit."

And that was that. The two, whatever they were, would put their recent sexual dalliances aside and concentrate on everything else. Somehow, that didn't make Loralin feel any better, but at least Devin was happy with it.

* * *

At noon, Loralin switched the open sign on and unlocked the main doors. Devin and the housekeeping staff were making sure the rest of the hotel and restaurant were accessible to patrons. The Only blemish on or in the rustic old building was the boarded-up window in room 322. It would be at least a week until the window casing could be rebuilt and the glass replaced.

Loralin had just hung up the phone from a conversation with the general contractor when there was a knock on the door. "Enter!"

Maureen poked her head in. "Deke Robertson is here, and he'd like to speak with you."

Deke Robertson was a snake in the grass who owned over half the hotels in Casper and was always on the lookout for troubled properties to take over. His methods were thought to be somewhat questionable. "What does he want?"

Maureen slipped into the room and quietly closed the door. "He won't say, but he looks as smarmy as ever. Should I tell him you're busy?"

With a sigh, Loralin stood, "No, he'll just keep making a nuisance of himself. Send him in."

There was only one thing that unnerved a man like Deke, and that was a woman in control. Instead of sitting back down, she leaned her butt against the desk and crossed her legs in front of her. He would have to remain standing for the visit.

"Loralin Robbins!" Deke said, showing his too-white-to-be-real toothy smile. "How have you been?"

"Fine, just fine," she answered with a small smile. "What can I do for you?"

Deke's eyes shot around the room, then back to Loralin. She knew he'd been sizing up his chances of sitting down. His face never showed it, but it was obvious that he was more uncomfortable than usual. "I just came to see how you're holding up after that tragic event this week."

Loralin laughed, letting him know she didn't buy into his bullshit. "Don't you mean you're here to see if, after two murders on the premises, I'm ready to turn tail and run so you can buy the place cheap?"

"I should be offended," he finally said after anger had flashed across his face. He was slipping up in his old age. "Can't a man show concern for a fellow hotelier?"

"Most men can," she ground out. "But not you, Deke. I'm going to tell you exactly what my grandfather told you. This inn is not for sale to anyone, especially you."

The man held up his hands in surrender. "Okay, okay, no

reason to get snippy about it. I'll drop it for now and just ask if you have a room available for me for a week and a meeting room, I could book for two days. I'm conducting business in the area, and with the detours because of the flood, I'd hate to have to travel back and forth."

Loralin thought about it for a moment, making him wait. On one hand, they could use the business, and he was known for being a good tipper. But on the other hand, he had to be up to something, and she wasn't sure if she had the energy to fight him off. She had to remember that she wasn't alone in this adventure, though. She had Devin and the best crew in the world. "We can accommodate your request." She stood up straight and moved close to him. "But if I find out you are scheming or conniving to sabotage my inn, you'll be out on your ass and in a courtroom before you even catch your breath."

Deke had the good grace not to say anything except, "Thank you, Loralin."

Turning to her desk, she pressed a button on the phone. "Maureen, I'm sending Mr. Robertson out there. He wishes to make a reservation and book a meeting room."

After picking up the same invoice for the third or fourth time, Loralin put it in her folder and shoved it in her drawer. Having Deke Robertson in-house was worrisome. He'd tried to trick her grandparents more than once and had almost succeeded while her grandmother was on her deathbed. It was time to rally the troops. She pressed a button on the phone again. "Devin, organize a staff meeting with everyone, even those not on duty. ASAP!"

* * *

"Okay, boss, the staff meeting is scheduled for two p.m. Everyone on shift will gather in here, and the rest will join us via video on Boom.

Loralin finally felt like she could start to relax again. "Thank you. We'll soon have Deke neutralized, and then I can concentrate on other things".

"Is he really that conniving?" Devin had only met the man once or twice, briefly.

"Oh yes," Loralin said, leaning back in her chair and closing her eyes. "He's been said to have released various critters into hotel rooms and dining rooms. Hell, one hotel in Casper claims he poisoned their continental breakfast with laxatives. And that doesn't include all of the legal maneuverings and loopholes he tries to use to take people's livelihoods.

"So, what's the plan, then?" Devin never got his answer because employees invaded the room in small groups until they were all there. And with the click of a couple of buttons on a keyboard, the staff who had been scheduled off that day were joining them.

Once everyone was present and logged in, Loralin stood and motioned for attention. "Okay, guys, I called this meeting because there is a possible enemy in our midst and I need help from each and every one of you to keep him neutralized."

Whispers ripped through the room. Some knew who the person was, while others didn't. Loralin continued, "Mr. Deke Robertson is a guest who will be with us for a week. I want him treated just like any other guest. However, I also want all of you to keep your ears and eyes open. If you notice anything out of the ordinary, especially something that could be detrimental to this inn, you are to report it to Devin or me immediately.

More whispers circled the room and came from the computer speakers. Devin stood and took over for Loralin. "Okay, everybody, if you love this place and your jobs, keep vigilant. Now back to work!"

* * *

Once everyone was gone, Loralin sat in her chair, and Devin sat across the desk from her. He could tell she was getting antsy, most likely about the case. "Have you heard from Heather? Shouldn't she have been here by now?"

"Oh, I forgot to tell you," she said with a yawn. "She had to run back to Casper to get some stuff. She'll come over for dinner tonight, and we can strategize after."

Devin was a bit relieved. He had people to train, and if Heather had shown up, he'd have had to put it off. His new hires were eager to get started despite the recent murder. "That sounds good. I'm going to go start orientation. I'll meet you at the house sometime after five."

As Devin gathered the three new hires in the lobby, an idea hit him and wouldn't let go. The week before the murder, he'd trained eight new people. What if one of them had murdered Phyllis? Even Loralin had said she didn't recognize most of them. He would grab their files before he headed home so they could look them over. Maybe one of them matched a name from Phyllis's past. He was no true detective, but he knew they followed their gut, and his gut was telling him that someone local, someone they knew and cared about and had been displaced by the flood, could not have killed the woman. It seemed to him that the murder was almost a crime of passion and extreme anger, not a crime done out of momentary anger at a known instigator.

He had to laugh at himself. Just a month or so before, he would never have known the difference between a crime done out of deep emotions and one done in the spur of the moment. But whoever had killed Phyllis had wrapped their hands around her throat until she stopped breathing, and it hadn't been enough. They'd had to pick her up and throw her with mighty force out the window to watch her body break on the ground. Whoever killed Phyllis had hated her with a thousand points of passion and anger. And he knew that Loralin would agree.

* * *

Loralin and Heather were just setting the table when Devin walked in. "Wow, something sure smells good," he enthused.

"Heather stopped at Mabel's Diner and got us some takeout so we wouldn't have to cook."

"I figured you were probably as tired as I am," Heather said with a smile. "I hope you still like a hamburger with the works and hot chips."

"I do." Devin headed to the sink to wash his hands. "I'm surprised you remembered."

"You guys were friends for years. You've gotten to know each other pretty well," Loralin reminded him. Sometimes she still wondered if they had had feelings for each other, but knew it would never work because of the distance. Apparently, her close bond and friendship with her daughter's friend hadn't been an issue because they knew they would never love each other. But because of all that, she wasn't sure how the young woman would react if she knew they had slept together. For now, it would be a secret because it may never happen again.

The three gathered at the dinner table and dug into the food made at the best restaurant in town. Mable's was known statewide for the best home cooking in the Western half of the country.

Loralin handed out papers that she'd printed off from the information she'd uploaded from Miles's tablet when Heather had arrived an hour earlier. "I can't believe your dad trusted you with his work tablet."

"He didn't have much choice," Heather interjected. "Tonight is his and Meredith's second anniversary. He had to take her out for a special dinner and couldn't come with me."

Devin had been ignoring Loralin and Heather. He was more interested in what the pages he held had to say. "So, there have been a total of five incidents where people have blamed Phyllis for the death or injury of a child or mother. None of them went far as the hospitals paid them off."

"How was she still a nurse?" Loralin mumbled around a bite of her chicken-fried steak. "I would have fired her long ago."

"She would switch hospitals after a couple of incidents," Heather murmured. "This is all the information we went to Tanner Health with when they took over the hospital and needed a new labor and delivery head."

"And they just ignored it?" Devin huffed. "I can't believe that."

"That's corporate America for you," Loralin said. "They could promote Phyllis thousands of dollars cheaper than if they'd had to hunt for someone outside the hospital to take the position."

Devin was still shaking his head when Loralin got up and went to the refrigerator. "I don't know about the rest of you, but I'm starving. I'm having my dessert now. Anyone else?"

Both of the others agreed that they wanted their desserts too, so Loralin grabbed all three pieces of Mabel's famous cheesecake and brought them to the table. "So, are there any names involved in the complaints about Phyllis that are the same as any of the out-of-town guests we had during the flood?"

Heather and Devin both told her there weren't, and all three of them were quiet while they ate their dessert.

"Did you have IDs for any of the stranded guests?" Heather asked. "I mean, if I were going to commit murder, I surely wouldn't check in under my own name."

"We did check them in as if they were planned guests. We can check that tomorrow," Loralin said. "And we can get your father to check them out and make sure they all were who they said they were."

After more silence and eating, Devin remembered what he'd been thinking about earlier. "Hey," he said reluctantly, still unsure of his talents as an amateur sleuth. "What about all the newbies we hired last week? There were only a couple that were known to you, Loralin. The rest were from Boone or new in town. Should we have Miles check them out, too?"

"I taught him well," Loralin said, putting a sweet, slow kiss on his lips. It wasn't until Heather cleared her throat and laughed that she realized what she'd done right in front of her daughter. "I uh... well, anyway, I think it's a great idea to have them checked out. Are they all still working for us?"

"Yes," Devin answered. "As of today, they are all still with us. We'll have to keep an eye on that over the next week or so."

"So," Heather said as she stood and started to clear the few dishes they had used. "I guess there isn't much investigating to do until you talk to Daddy."

Loralin jumped up and started helping her daughter load the dishwasher. "Yeah. It's so frustrating. I feel like we should have a suspect to question by now."

"You could always talk to Chef. He had more reason to want her dead than I did. And from what I hear, he had about ten to fifteen minutes unaccounted for when he went to the bathroom right before breakfast was served."

"Oh, not again," Devin said with a groan. "Chef is completely off his rocker, but he's not a murderer. When we questioned him last time, I felt like such a bad person for doing so."

"I know," Loralin agreed. "But we have to question everyone, and Heather is right, he had a motive."

Once the dishes were put in the dishwasher, Heather called it a night and left the two alone. "You up for a movie tonight?" Loralin asked. "I was thinking something with a character named Nurse Ratched might be fun."

"Ooh," Devin said with a laugh. "I've never seen *One Flew Over the Cuckoo's Nest*! I'll go get ready for bed and meet you in the living room."

Even though Lorlin thought it was probably for the best that they kept it casual in the living room, she was also somewhat disappointed. Sex with Devin was amazing, but it was also way too complicated at the moment.

8

Sleuth Loralin Rides at Dawn

When Loralin woke up on the couch fully clothed, she was alone. Devin had either gone to his room sometime during the night, or he was already at work. The phone ringing gave her the answer. It was Devin. "Hey, where are you?"

"At the inn. There was a problem with one of the washing machines, so when the call came in, I decided to let you sleep and come down to handle it. Will you be here soon? Miles is coming to meet with us in about an hour."

"Um… Yeah, I'll be there as soon as I can."

"Great," he said. "Don't forget the files."

While Loralin showered, she went over how different this case was to the previous one; not the murder itself, but Devin's reaction to it and his willingness to sleuth. She knew he still sometimes worried about what they were getting into, but more often than not, he was enjoying the hell out of himself. She hoped he realized how difficult this one was going to be to solve because he could easily get disenchanted if it took too long or if he had to do too many things that made him uncomfortable.

When she stepped out of the shower, she heard her text tone go off, so she quickly dried her hands and opened the message. "Hurry the hell up. :)" It was from Devin.

* * *

As Loralin walked down the path to the inn, she saw Miles coming from the other direction. She waited for him by the front doors. "Any news from forensics yet?" It was a bit early, but she still hoped he had something.

"Just that there were no usable prints on the window casing or glass fragments. And there were prints from the housekeepers, room service employees, and the three people staying in the room all over the place. "So, you're saying that the fingerprint evidence is going to get us nowhere?"

"Yep."

Miles walked alongside Loralin to her office, where Devin waited for them. "Good morning," he said to the young man.

"Morning," Devin said with a smile. "We've got some work for you, sir. Are you up for it?"

Loralin looked at her ex-husband and couldn't tell if he was going to groan or gladly accept the assignment. "We need you to look into all of the out-of-town guests that were here during the flood and some of our newest employees. None of their names matched any of the complaints filed about Phyllis, so we want to make sure these people are who they said they are."

"That's easy," Miles said, looking relieved. "Sargent Linda Henderson is going to be helping me a bit. I'm going to try to keep her in the dark about you helping out, but who knows if it will work."

"So, how long do you think it will take to get some information on these people?" Loralin asked.

"Give me a few days," Miles offered. "In the meantime, if you happen to be working and can question people here at the inn, I won't complain."

Devin and Loralin smiled at each other. It was game on. "Let the sleuthing begin," he said. "First up is Mr. Phyllis Palmer, otherwise known as Chef Pierre."

"Did I just hear my name?" came a booming voice from the doorway.

"Ah, Chef, yes, we wanted to talk to you." Loralin walked over to him and took his arm to escort him to a seat at the meeting table in the corner.

"I'll show myself out," Miles murmured and closed the door behind him.

"So, what did you want to speak to me about?" the old chef said with a flourish.

"We just want to make sure you're holding up okay," Loralin said kindly. "You know, since it was your ex-wife who died."

The old man's usually pleasant, plump face grimaced and turned red. "Why on earth wouldn't I be okay? That woman was the devil, and she has now been vanquished from this earth."

"Oh, come on, Pierre," Devin said in a quiet voice. "You don't want to talk like that where people might hear. Look what happened to poor Heather."

"Oh, I didn't kill the old bat. She was the biggest mistake of my life, but I didn't see her that much. Since she moved out of town, I rarely saw her. Besides, I have an alibi!" He was now dead serious with no flare or anger, a side you didn't often see from him.

"Oh?" Loralin said nonchalantly. "You were fixing breakfast for the restaurant, weren't you?"

"Yes, and then I went to the men's room, where I was texting my friend in Boone. I hardly think I could kill a woman and throw her out a window while texting someone."

"Wow, lucky you were texting your friend," Devin sympathized. "Otherwise, they may have tried to pin it on you."

The chef huffed. "No offense, Loralin, but knowing that bumbling police department, I'm surprised they didn't haul me in right alongside your Heather."

"None taken," she chuckled. "My ex-husband and his fellow officers get a little bit off-kilter sometimes."

"To say the least," he growled. "I'm so glad that idiot ex-husband of yours lets you help. Otherwise, half the town would be in jail for crimes they didn't commit."

Loralin had to admit that she felt a bit offended now. Her ex was a good guy, and he did the best he could with what he had. He was a smart man. But it wasn't worth arguing about. "Oh, one other thing, Chef. I'd appreciate it if you didn't try to steal people from the hotel to work in the kitchen in the future. If you are shorthanded, let us know, and we'll let you hire someone."

"Fair enough," the old man said as he rose from his seat. "I'll need one more cook. I have someone in mind. Is it alright if I hire him?"

"I trust your judgment," Loralin said. "Do what you need to do." With a quick nod, he turned and left the room.

Devin headed toward the door himself. "I'm going to work the desk. If you need me, holler."

"Will do. I'll compile a list of people I think we should talk to." Loralin already had her head buried in the files about the case.

"Let's be a little more discreet about it with other people than we were with Chef." Devin was always afraid that he would offend someone or make an enemy. Loralin had no such fear. The people in this town knew how she was, and the people who weren't from Elk River didn't matter one bit.

* * *

The next two days went quickly as Devin and Loralin split her list and questioned everyone who worked in the inn. They found nothing useful until they came to the last two people on the list. All of a sudden, about a week after the murder, two of their newer employees stopped showing up for work.

"So, Zoey Workman, 23 years old, lives in Boone, and Hank Perkins, 25 years old, also lives in Boone?" Loralin asked.

"Yeah, they were scheduled yesterday and didn't show up. Then today they didn't show up either, and when I called their phone numbers, neither was in service."

"Well, that doesn't look suspicious," Lorlain snickered. "I wonder what they are or were up to. Did they seem associated?"

"Yeah, they both asked to be housekeepers because they were best friends and wanted to work together." Devin handed their personnel files to his boss.

"You know what, I'm thinking I'd like to have a night out. I hear that the new bar and grill, you know the one that just moved into the spot where the other one used to be, is a pretty happening place these days. I wonder if anyone there knows our two former housekeepers?"

"Ah, great idea. Batista's Bar and Grill in Boone for a late dinner and drinks tonight, it is." Devin seemed excited by the prospect. "And by the way, before we get there and have to act like we know what we're talking about, umm… we young people don't say a place is 'happening' anymore. That's kind of an old lady term."

The pen that Loralin threw at him barely missed his head and dropped to the ground. "Go on, brat. We'll talk later."

"Love you, bestie," he crooned.

"Love you too, pain in my ass."

Devin might not know what he wanted from her, but it didn't seem to affect the solid base they already had. He still seemed to love teasing her about her age. If anybody else had called her an old lady, she might have let them have it, but since it was Devin, it was just a normal part of who they were.

She'd almost reminded him that she didn't act like much of an old lady when they were having sex. But she had promised to give him time to figure out what to do about their relationship, and she was determined to stick to it.

* * *

The half-hour drive to Boone felt so much like normal to Loralin. That in itself caused her much stress. Did that mean that they were destined to be only friends, that things were just more comfortable that way? And if so, why did she care so much? That ride, with him at the wheel and her chattering in the passenger seat, was the first time she realized that if their relationship did change, it meant that they loved each other.

Not just friend love but LOVE love. Did she have feelings for him? Who was she kidding? She did have feelings for him, but what could she do about it? She could go with it and hope for the best, or she could ignore them completely. Deciding which one to choose was her problem at the moment. She didn't want to be the only one in love. How embarrassing would that be, an old lady falls in love with a young stud, and he laughs at her for thinking it was possible for someone like him to love someone like her. Yep, it was best to stop thinking about it. In this case, he might just have to make the first move if there was a move to be made.

"Have you heard if the food is any good?" Loralin finally asked to break the silence.

"I've heard it's better than what was there before. And the drinks are cheaper." Devin concentrated on the road as he drove Loralin's SUV down the lonely highway between the two towns. There wasn't much along the way except plains.

"Well, at least we will get some good food and cheap drinks out of it. I'm not feeling like this is a good idea anymore." She didn't dare look at him; she knew what she'd see in his eyes.

Devin took his eyes off the road long enough to throw Loralin an exasperated look. "Should I turn around?"

"No. Let's just do it and get it over with. If it turns out to be a waste of time, then at least we had a nice evening away from home." She couldn't define what she was feeling. She wasn't sure if it was fear of what they would find out, or who they might piss off, or if it was that they were looking at this all wrong.

Devin pulled into the parking lot of Batista's Bar and Grill. It was a Friday night, and they were busy. "I sure hope the wait isn't too long. I didn't have lunch."

Loralin put her hand over her stomach. "Same here. I'm so hungry all of a sudden."

Devin had left the car and was opening her door for her. "It's because you can smell the food cooking. Damn, that has to be some good food!"

The aroma was even more intoxicating when they stepped inside. "Hello," said the sweet hostess from her position behind a small counter. "Two of you tonight?"

"Yes," Loralin answered. "Can we order food at the bar?"

"Absolutely," the young woman answered. "Our bar is first-come, first-served. You can go see if you can find seats. If you change your mind and want to sit in the dining area, just let me know."

Devin nodded to the girl and put his hand on Loralin's back, guiding her over to the bar where he'd spied two seats together, in the middle of all the action.

"What can I get ya to drink?" the bartender asked as he dried his hands on a towel.

"I'll have a beer," Loralin said.

"Same here," Devin agreed. "Give us whatever you've got on tap."

When the bartender brought them their drinks, he also had two menus with him. "You gonna eat too?"

"Yes, thank you," Loralin said, reaching for the menus.

"Yup," the man mumbled. "Your server will be over in just a moment. "

It wasn't long before their order was in the kitchen, and they set about watching the people around them, hoping they'd get lucky and see the two people they were looking for. By the time their food arrived, they agreed that their former employees weren't at the bar that night.

"Can I get you another beer?" The bartender asked Devin when he noticed his empty glass.

"Uh… yeah. Go ahead and bring her another one, too." Loralin was drinking much more slowly than he had, but he figured it was best not to run out. "I'll ask the bartender if he knows them. You want to go catch the server?"

"Yep," Loralin agreed and took two big swigs of her beer. "Don't drink my new one while I'm gone," she teased.

The bartender brought the two beers as soon as he'd poured them. "Here you go. Anything else?"

"Actually, I wonder if you could help me out with some information. I'm looking for a couple of old friends who seem to have gone missing." He held out the employee pictures he had in his hand.

"Yeah, that looks like Zoey and Hank. I haven't seen them since they took off for Elk River to work at that new inn, the one with all the murders."

"Oh," Devin said, his surprise showing. "They moved down there?"

"Yup," the man answered. "They got kicked out of their place here, so they moved down there and got the job to start over fresh."

"Okay, I guess I'll have to go look there. Thank you," Devin wasn't exactly happy with the amount of information he got, but at least it was something.

"Hey, I may have hit the jackpot," Loralin said as she sat down and finished off her first beer, then exchanged it for the second one.

"Oh?"

"Yeah, the waitress went to school with them. According to her, they aren't best friends; they are married. They get kicked out of places a lot, and they go through jobs so quickly that they moved on to Elk River just to be able to work."

"Yeah, the bartender said they had moved to Elk River." He sounded disappointed that she had the same information as she did.

"But that's not the best part," Loralin said, noticing his disappointed demeanor. "It seems that Zoey's little sister died fifteen years ago at the hands of a nurse she always described as having an evil bedside manner and being incompetent."

Devin hit the counter with his fist. "Well, I'll be damned, that sounds a lot like our dear departed friend Phyllis."

"Yep," Loralin agreed. "I think we should celebrate with some dessert and another beer, and in the morning, we can call Miles and let him investigate the situation. There has to be a paper trail to Phyllis somewhere."

"Or we could finish up these beers, head home, and try digging through the paperwork to find a connection now," Devin offered, knowing what she would choose.

"Now that sounds like a fun night," Loralin said with a laugh. "You square up the bill, and I'll go to the bathroom, and we'll meet at the exit." Devin nodded his consent and motioned for the bartender.

* * *

Loralin sat at the dining room table, poring over the files about Phyllis. While Devin made them some coffee. "I just don't see anything. None of the last names match. Unless Zoey was married before. Of course, I've ruled out the two families with boy babies since it was her sister who died."

"I think I'm going to reread the complaints against her and see if anything fits." Devin put Loralin's coffee in front of her and sat down with his mug. "I know there was a case where a woman said she felt like the baby was coming, so her husband called Phyllis, the nurse on duty, and she didn't respond for twenty minutes. By then, the baby's head was out, and the cord was wrapped around the neck. Because Phyllis didn't respond immediately to check the woman and call the doctor, by the time he arrived, the baby had been strangled by its own cord. Phyllis said that the call button must not have worked, but when they checked it later that day, it was working just fine."

"Jesus," Loralin ground out. "Heather always told me that Phyllis only did things on her own time. She'd leave patients needing things until it suited her to take care of them."

Devin looked up from the file he was reading. "The only reason it didn't go to court was that the hospital shifted the blame to the husband for not leaving her bedside to fetch the nurse. And the only reason the hospital paid out a cash settlement is that the family's attorney argued that the baby hadn't crowned until right before Phyllis came in, so there was no reason until that point for the husband to rush out and find someone to help."

"And this one here," Loralin said, sifting through her papers, "was a case where the mother's blood pressure spiked, and the baby's heart rate dropped. Phyllis had determined that the monitor wasn't working, but hadn't replaced it with one that did. It wasn't until the mother went into convulsions that the husband noticed something was wrong and went to get Phyllis. By then, it was too late. Both mother and baby died."

"Damn," Devin murmured.

Loralin nodded her agreement and continued. "Once again,

the hospital tried to pin the blame on the husband, and the lawyer argued that the husband couldn't have known what went wrong. They settled this case, too. This was at the regional hospital in Boone. Shortly after that, Phyllis moved to the hospital in Casper."

Devin felt sick to his stomach. How many lives had this woman so blatantly thrown away? "Did the server say whether Zoey had lost her mother, too?"

"No," Loralin said with a sigh. "All she remembered was the baby. But I guess anything is possible."

"So, we're stuck again, then," Devin said. He felt so useless. The person who killed Phyllis needed to be found and given a medal.

"Maybe not," Loralin said as she shuffled more papers. "The attorney who handled both cases happens to be my attorney. I'm going to meet with him and see if he knows Zoey."

"Ooh, a bit of luck finally! But that's only four babies accounted for. What about the fifth?"

Loralin moved some papers aside and picked up one to read. "Couldn't be that baby. This happened about a year ago, and Zoey's baby sister died fifteen years ago."

"Okay then. Hopefully, the attorney can meet with you tomorrow." Devin was suddenly tired and was thinking about turning in for the night.

"I won't give him a choice," Loralin chuckled. "I'll show up at his office when he gets there at 8:30. Want to come with me?"

"You know I do." He kissed her on the head and turned to leave the room. "I'm exhausted. Goodnight, Loralin."

"Night," she said quietly. He hadn't even stayed long enough for her to ask if he wanted to watch a show. Was he avoiding the subject, or was he just that tired? It turned out it was neither of those as she learned at about one a.m.

* * *

Devin couldn't sleep, no matter how tired he felt. He kept tossing and turning and thinking of all of the lives that Phyllis had been allowed to ruin. It was just so sad and nauseating. What he really needed was someone to talk to. Loralin was that someone, and he hoped she wouldn't mind being woken up.

"Loralin, are you awake?" he asked quietly.

"No," she returned and sat up to turn on the bedside light. "What's up?"

"What Phyllis did to those poor families just keeps running through my mind. I can't shake it." He sat down on the bed by Loralin's legs and rubbed his hand up and down one of them.

"Same here," she said. "I haven't been to sleep yet."

"How could someone do that and let the hospital blame the families and then keep doing it over and over again?" Why did he feel like he wanted to cry all of a sudden? He knew he wouldn't, but he also knew he was safe in her presence.

"That's the way Phyllis was. She was bullied and never batted an eye or cried or anything. It was like she was a robot. The only thing that made her feel was Miles, and then she lost him to me." Loralin reached up to caress his face. She heard a little gasp and encouraged him to move closer.

Devin knew immediately what she wanted, and he gave it to her. His lips met hers, and they melted together, all their feelings of sadness and anger coming out in that one kiss. "God, I love kissing you, Loralin."

"You're the best kisser I've ever met," she whispered before kissing him again. "Devin, can we…"

"I need you right now. It feels like the only thing that can take this horrible feeling away is to be buried deep inside of you."

"Then what are you waiting for?" Loralin knew in that instant that what they had, what they *both* felt, was more than just friendship. But she was too scared to face it herself. Devin would have to be the one to decide the time was right to try life as lovers. She had always readily admitted that she was a coward in love.

* * *

The cloudy, humid morning brought another trip to Boone. Jackson Fairway, Attorney at Law, was based in the largest town in the county, and he practiced all over the middle part of the state. He had been Loralin's attorney since he helped her with the probate of her inheritance from her grandparents.

"I hope this guy can help with some information," Devin said from the passenger seat. "I feel kind of bad that we haven't told Miles about the two missing employees yet."

"Oh, he knows," Loralin said. "Heather told him, and he is also doing some digging if he gets time. The Chief has him escorting a felon to Cheyenne. He won't be back in town until later tonight."

Devin snorted in disgust. "I'm surprised the town hasn't gotten rid of that no-good chief. There's a murder that needs to be solved for Cripe's sake. The town's only detective needs to be working on that, not escorting a prisoner."

"I know," Loralin agreed. "Nobody within the department likes him, but the powers that be couldn't get rid of him, so they promoted him to a place where they thought he would turn tail and run. Unfortunately, everyone in Elk River PD is afraid to cross him, and he loves the power he has over them."

"Maybe this case will backfire on him," Devin said with genuine hope in his voice. "And he will retire."

Loralin shrugged. "We can always hope."

* * *

Jackson Fairway had a quaint little office on the main street. It had once been a small house. "I love these old buildings with the gingerbread trim," said Devin.

"I thought you'd like it," Loralin said with a smile. Devin had always loved old architecture. She figured that was why he'd always liked the inn so much, even before she restored and reopened it.

Devin pulled the door open, letting Loralin precede him into the room. A bell above the door jingled. There was no one sitting at the receptionist's desk, but they heard movement in the office behind it.

"Hello," came a voice that Loralin had only been able to describe as 'smooth as butter.' "Loralin Robbins! It's great to see you."

"Likewise, Jackson," she returned. "I was wondering if we could have just a minute or two of your time before your first appointment."

The man smiled and motioned for them to enter his office. "You can have more than that. My first appointment was canceled; hence the reason Joyce wasn't out there to properly greet you."

Once they were settled, Loralin pulled papers out of the soft-sided briefcase she was carrying. "I'm sure you heard we had a murder the other day at my inn. Within the week, we had two employees disappear on us, and we are trying to see what connection they may have had to the victim."

"I just returned from Tahiti last night," he said, his voice unable to hide his surprise. "Who was murdered this time?"

Devin cleared his throat. "Phyllis Palmer."

"Well, I'll be damned," Jackson murmured. "Karma finally got the old bat."

"Yep," Loralin agreed. "Fifteen years ago or so, you handled two wrongful death suits against her, and we just need to know if the missing young lady is associated with either family. We do know that at about that time, this young lady lost a sister at birth."

"Okay," Jackson said, grabbing his glasses from the desktop and putting them on. "What information do you have on her?"

"Her name is Zoey Workman," Loralin said. "And this is what she looks like now." She pushed the personnel file she'd brought across the desk to him.

With a sigh, Jackson opened the folder and then closed it before taking his glasses off. "Yeah, Zoey lost her baby sister at the hands of Phyllis Palmer. I represented her mother and father in the case. This was a particularly sad one."

"What do you mean?" Devin questioned.

"About a year after the death, Zoey lost both parents to suicide. I guess they just couldn't take the loss of their baby girl. And it didn't help that Phyllis stood up in mediation and blamed the man for his own child's death. Zoey was eventually adopted by the Workmans and did okay until she graduated from high school. She's been scraping by ever since."

Loralin thought she heard a deep growl coming from beside her. When she turned to look at Devin, she could see the anger in his eyes. "You okay?"

"Yeah," he murmured angrily. "I swear if that woman hadn't been killed already, I'd do it myself."

"I'll tell you one thing," Jackson said, laying his glasses back on his desk. "You know, you hear people talking about pure evil? Well, Phyllis was the epitome of pure evil. Most people thought she was just a bitch, but she had a heart of stone and a conniving, manipulative mind that ruined a lot of people's lives over the years. "

Those words chilled Loralin to the bone. Why hadn't she ever come after her? She was the one person in the world that Phyllis hated the most. Had she planned on getting to her through Heather? Would ruining her daughter's career have been the sweetest revenge against losing Miles? It took thirty miles of staring out the passenger window as the plains rolled by to tuck away the sick feeling she'd had in Jackson Fairway's office. For the first time ever, she was truly, one hundred percent glad that someone was dead, and she didn't like feeling that way. She'd been brought up to think everyone had a good side. Her parents and grandparents had been dead wrong in that assumption.

9

Emotional Rollercoasters

Arriving back at the house, Devin parked under the carport and turned to Loralin. "You okay?"

"Yeah. I mean, I will be." She shrugged and reached for the door handle.

"What happened back there, Loralin? You're not leaving this car until you tell me."

"Can we talk about it later, please?" She felt like she would cry at any moment. I'm not feeling very well. Go ahead and go to work. I'll check in later. I think I need the day off."

"I'm not going anywhere," he insisted. "I'll call Maureen and Gage and make sure things are running smoothly, and we'll both take the day off."

He was out of the car and on his phone before Loralin could argue about it. She was too tired to argue anyway, so she headed inside to set about making lunch for her and Devin. After that, she wanted to sleep, a blissful, healing sleep.

"I could have made us lunch," Devin said when he walked in the back door. "Why don't you sit down, and I'll get us some drinks. I'd really like to hear what went on back there."

Loralin nodded her consent for him to take over, and she took the sandwiches to the table, where she sat down and started to unburden herself to her biggest confidant. She told him of the fear she had about Phyllis's plans for Heather. She told them how awful it felt to truly be happy that someone had their life snuffed out. She told him how much it had jarred her to find out that someone she thought was harmless and annoying was actually evil and conniving enough to be murdered. And then once lunch was cleared away, and she was lying in bed next to Devin watching one of their shows, she cried. When she woke up nearly two hours later, he was still holding her as he had when she'd cried herself to sleep.

"Hey," he said when she stirred beside him. "Feel any better?"

"Yeah," she whispered. "I'm sorry I got so emotional."

Devin lifted her chin so she was looking at him. "Don't apologize. Ever. You know better."

He was right; they had agreed to never apologize for needing support from each other. That's what best friends were for. "Okay. Do you know what time it is?"

"Half past four," he said, picking up his phone to look at the time. "I know what you're thinking, but Miles won't be home until later, so don't go watching the clock waiting for him."

Loralin laughed. "I didn't plan on it. He has hands free on his cell phone. I figured I'd call him while he drives home."

Devin laughed with her. "I always thought I was the one with no patience, but it turns out that's you."

"Hey," Loralin said, swatting his arm. "Old ladies are always patient. It's young bucks like you that have no patience."

"Young Buck?" His eyebrow raised, and he was trying not to burst out laughing. "I never quite thought of myself as a young buck."

"Well, Loralin said, sitting up in bed. "You are living in Wyoming now, so young buck kinda fits. Unless you want me to call you a young ass. You'd be surprised how many donkeys we have here…" She let her voice trail off.

"I'll take 'young buck,'" he finally agreed. "I can't believe you called me an ass."

"I'll stop calling you an ass if you stop calling me old," she teased.

"Well, shit. I'm not so sure I can do that, so I guess I'm going to have to get used to being called an ass."

"Ugh!" Loralin roared playfully. "You are impossible."

"Yeah," he said, moving to the edge of the bed to sit by her. "And sitting here with you, in your bed, it's impossible not to want to kiss you."

"Then go ahead," she breathed.

Devin's lips met Loralin's for the briefest of moments before he pulled away, groaned as if in pain, and fled into the hallway. "Sorry," he said softly. I thought I could do this, but it just won't work. It's wrong."

Loralin was shocked, to say the least. Just the night before, he'd come to her, and they'd taken comfort in each other. What on earth had happened in the last fourteen hours or so? Had she become too needy with her feelings on the Phyllis situation? Was her being happy that Phyllis was dead scaring him? It wasn't until she got up and walked into the bathroom that she remembered hearing him talking to someone while she was dozing in his arms. His mother. His mother had called him. No wonder he was pulling away. Despite how horrid she'd been to him, he always wanted her approval, and she would never approve of our relationship, whether just friends or something more, and she'd gone to desperate lengths to prove it.

* * *

Devin reappeared at five o'clock after locking himself in his room. "I have an idea for dinner tonight, if you're up to it, that is." He couldn't bring himself to look directly at her. After everything that happened and his words to her, he felt uncomfortable. It was best just to act as if nothing had happened.

"I'm feeling pretty good," she admitted. Even though she felt a little bit like her heart was about to break. "What do you have in mind?"

"How about we barbecue steaks, make some potato salad, and garlic bread. We can invite my dad and brother, your daughters, and Meredith, and Miles can join us when he gets home. That way you won't have to call him while he's driving."

"It would be hands-free," she murmured. "But yeah, he could get in trouble with the chief if he talked while driving on duty. Let's do it."

"Okay then. I'll call everyone and then come help you with the food." What had happened with his mother when he moved to America still weighed on his mind sometimes, but when he had Loralin's family and friends around him, he almost felt whole again. He almost felt like he belonged, and tonight was one of those nights where he needed to feel that sense of family.

* * *

"Hey, Dad!" Devin said as he opened the door to the inn's head of maintenance and hugged him. "Trevor, are you behaving?" He and his little brother had always been close, and he and his dad were getting along better than ever since his mother left the picture.

"Of course I am," Trevor said, his face turning red. "I never get to see you anymore, though."

Devin felt bad that his little brother now lived in town with their dad, and they couldn't hang out like they used to. "Just call, and we'll come get you," he said.

"Or come to work with your dad, and you two can hang out at the inn," Loralin said as she walked up behind them.

Devin smiled appreciatively at his boss. There were perks to being in good standing with the owner. "Come on in, guys. Dinner is just about ready."

Before they could get the front door closed, Loralin's daughters and Meredith showed up. "Have you guys heard from Miles? I can't reach him on the phone." His wife looked a little bit frantic.

"I haven't tried," Loralin said. "Come on into the living room, and we can call him again."

While the ladies went to try to get a hold of Miles, Devin, and his dad and brother headed to the kitchen to gather the steaks and take them out to the back patio, where the grill was burning hot and waiting. "Still loving your new job, Dad?" Devin asked.

"You know I am," the older man said with a smile that didn't quite reach his eyes.

"Hey Trevor," Devin said quietly. "Could you run inside and grab me the red bowl out of the refrigerator? Be careful because it's liquid and will spill easily."

Once Trevor was gone, Devin turned to his dad. "What's wrong, Dad? You aren't having second thoughts about selling our hotel and moving here to America, are you?"

"Oh, hell no," the old man grumbled. "It's just... You know how my mother left us when I was just a little kid?"

"Yeah..." Now, Devin was intrigued.

"Well, she contacted me and said she wants to see us. She wants to meet her grandchildren before she dies."

Devin's head spun. He truly never thought he'd meet the woman who birthed his father. "I'm guessing she's sick?"

"She is," Mark Wentworth whispered on an exhale. "Cancer. They've given her six months to live."

"Damn," Devin murmured, not quite sure what to say. "Are... are you thinking about going?"

Mark shrugged. "I want to. I think I need closure. But I also want you to come."

Devin accepted the red bowl from Trevor, who had suddenly reappeared. He used the brush inside to coat the steaks in his mom's special homemade steak sauce. "I could try to arrange that. Especially if this murder is solved quickly. Could I invite Loralin? She's always wanted to see the place I called home for my whole life."

"Yes," Mark said with a smile that finally reached his eyes. "I was going to suggest it myself. I think maybe you two would benefit from the trip. Maybe come to your senses about what's really going on."

Devin nearly dropped the red bowl, so he handed it off to Trevor to sit on the nearby patio table. "Please don't start with that, Dad. I'm confused enough as it is."

"I know," Mark said, his grin becoming the slightest bit mischievous. "I think the trip could help you and Loralin become unconfused."

Devin nodded slightly but didn't say anything. He didn't want to think about finding out stuff about him and Loralin. He wanted to solve the murder and go meet his paternal grandmother. It was unfortunate that deep down inside, he knew his dad was probably right. He desperately wanted to visit his home in Tasmania, but at the same time, he was afraid of what he'd find there if he did. His dad was counting on him, though, so he would do it.

* * *

Loralin hung up the phone when Miles didn't answer. His voicemail didn't even pick up. "I have an idea. I have a friend in the Cheyenne PD. I'll call him and ask if he knows where Miles is."

"Oh, you mean Mr. Handsy," Heather said. "He'll probably make you promise him a date before he'll give you any information."

Loralin knew her youngest was probably right. Don Peterson was a handsy little man, and he seemed to have a thing for her in particular. It probably had something to do with the fact that he and Miles were sworn enemies, but she didn't like to think about it much. And ever since the last murder, she had him on speed dial.

"This is Don Peterson." His voice was stoic and not animated like it usually was.

"Don, this is Loralin Robbins." She knew better than to say more because he always gushed over her immediately after she said her name.

"Loralin dear! To what do I owe the pleasure?" At least he sounded happier now.

"I'm calling to see if you've seen or heard from Miles. We've been trying to get a hold of him, and he doesn't answer, and his voicemail doesn't pick up."

"Well, I was hoping this was more of a personal call," he said in his smarmy teasing voice. "But yes, Miles is just fine. I think he was having issues with his voicemail notifications that were disrupting everything, so he turned it off."

"Oh, well, that's good to hear. Where exactly is he?" Meredith was sitting right next to her and looked relieved.

"Well, the prisoner that they transported here this morning escaped when he was being transferred from the station to the jail," Don admitted. Since he was the Chief of Police in Cheyenne, it was somewhat embarrassing for him. "So your Chief assigned Miles to stay and help. He said he was going to call his wife as soon as he could get a minute. But I wouldn't expect him home until late."

"Oh, okay. We're just glad he's okay. Thanks, Don. I owe you one." The minute the last four words slipped out of her mouth, she regretted it. Now he was going to call it in.

"Well," he drawled. "You could let me treat you to lunch when I'm there next week for the interview."

Loralin suddenly felt sick to her stomach. "Umm, interview?"

"Oh, I'm surprised you didn't hear!" Why did he sound like a child who had just gotten the best Christmas present ever? "I'm applying for Chief of Police in Elk River. It feels like I'm finally headed home. You know I started as a patrolman there."

Loralin knew very well. The hatred between her ex-husband and Don had started when they were partnered as detectives. "Well, uh... that's great news, Don. Best of luck." She was just about to hit end when his voice made her stop.

"So, what about lunch?"

Loralin was getting used to taking one for the team. "Oh sure, I'll have lunch with you, Don. Just let me know exactly when you plan to be here, and I'll make a reservation for us at The Pub. They've started serving lunch, and I hear it's great." She also knew how busy it was at lunchtime, so she wouldn't have to worry about Mr. Handsy getting too handsy.

With a satisfied "Great!" Don Peterson hung up the phone, and Loralin sank back into the couch cushions.

"Miles is safe, but he might be late. He has to chase an escapee thanks to the Chief."

"And what about Don Peterson?" Heather teased.

"It sounds like our current Chief of Police is leaving, and Don is applying for the opening."

All three of the other women burst into laughter, and after a moment of being offended, so did Loralin. It looked like life in Elk River could get interesting very soon.

* * *

By ten p.m., before everyone left Loralin's. Miles had called Meredith and apologized for not getting a hold of her sooner. But at least they'd caught their escapee. And he'd promised to talk to Loralin and Devin about Zoey first thing in the morning.

Once they'd bid farewell to their guests, Loralin and Devin settled onto the couch to watch a couple of episodes of their favorite comedy show. They usually did more talking than watching, though.

"I wonder why the Chief is leaving," Loralin said during an ad break. "I mean, I'm glad but... I'm not sure if I want Don Peterson to take over."

The look on Devin's face went from amusement to anger in a flash. "All I know is he'd better keep his paws off of you."

"Oh my God, you're jealous," she gasped, then grinned. There had been times when he'd acted like he didn't like her dating other people, but this time was different. He was actually angry.

"I am not!" His voice went high. "I couldn't care less who you date. I just don't like him as a person. He's gross."

"Right," she said with a laugh. "You are so jealous it isn't even funny. Do you love me, Devin?"

"Of course I do," he grumbled. "That's a stupid question. I loved you since before we first labeled our friendship."

"You know that's not what I meant," she snarled. "Are you in love with me, Devin?"

"I'm not jealous, damn it!" he growled back. "I just don't like the guy, and I don't want him making you uncomfortable."

"Right." This time her laugh lasted long enough that she felt Devin squirm in his seat.

"I'm going to bed," he said just loud enough for her to hear. He stood up, made his way past the couch, and headed down the hallway.

"Well, in that case, you won't mind that I'm having lunch with him on the day of his interview," she yelled after him. All she heard was a snarl and the slam of his bedroom door. It shook the whole house.

10

Who To Trust

Loralin and Devin didn't waste any time getting to work the next morning. And when Miles showed up at seven a.m., they all retired to her office.

"So, you are saying that someone who could have a motive for killing Phyllis gave you a false address and then quit working here a week after the murder?"

"Yes," Loralin said, turning her file over to her ex. Everyone in Boone said they'd moved to Elk River, but they gave us their last address in Boone."

"What were their alibis?" Devin asked. "I guess that's the first thing we should do to see if they can be ruled out."

"They said they were both at a bar out on State Route 247 until the last call and slept in their car in the parking lot. The morning bartender was pretty sure they'd been there when he came in to get ready for the day."

"Damn it," Devin said. "I had such high hopes for them being the murderers."

Miles looked at them. "Now that we know they disappeared, I think we should try to find them and re-question the bartender and people at the bar. There has to be a reason they suddenly disappeared. Right now, they are looking pretty damn guilty."

"Agreed," Loralin said. "We'll continue investigating the families that Phyllis ruined, and you can handle Zoey and Hank."

"Sounds good to me. You bring me suspects, and I investigate on behalf of the Elk River PD." Miles stood and was about to leave the room when Loralin stopped him.

"So, how do you feel about Chief Peterson possibly taking over for Chief Morris?"

Miles stopped in his tracks. "What did you just say?"

Devin chuckled and looked at Loralin. "I'm guessing he doesn't know."

Loralin burst into laughter. "I think Don is using me to do his dirty work. He could easily have told you while you were there yesterday."

"Son of a... I swear if that man becomes my boss, I'm looking for a new career." Miles's face was red with anger, and Loralin didn't think it would be a normal color for a long time. "I'll be in touch."

Loralin and Devin fought off belly laughs until he had shut the door behind him. Things were definitely going to get crazy in Elk River soon.

***

Loralin and Devin were both doing paperwork in her office when Lisa Marie, Devin's ex-girlfriend, knocked and stepped into the room. "Hey guys, can we talk for a minute?"

"Sure," Loralin said, putting the file she'd been looking at back on her desk. "What's up?"

"Well, you told us to keep an eye on Mr. Robertson…"

"Yes," Devin said, putting his papers back on the table in front of him. "What have you got?"

"Well, I don't know if it means anything, but I've seen the new guy, Jeremy, slipping into Mr. Robertson's room several times a day, and they were in the parking lot having a heated conversation when I left last night."

Devin stood up and moved to the supply closet, where he took out a notebook and a new pen. "I'm going to write down any instances that come to us."

"I wonder what's going on?" Loralin asked more to herself than to anyone else. "It could be something as innocent as them having an affair to something as sinister as working together to sabotage the Inn."

"That's what I was thinking," Lisa Marie said. "Is that the kind of information you were looking for?"

"Yes!" Loralin said, giving her a big smile. "Thanks for letting us know, and keep up the good work."

Once Lisa Marie was gone, Devin handed the notebook he had written in to Loralin. "So, what are your thoughts?"

She had been chewing on the end of her pen and finally took it out of her mouth and set it on the desk. "Well, I know for a fact that Mr. Robertson is a known ladies' man, but he could also have a thing for young men. My gut tells me they might just be up to no good, though."

Devin agreed. "I think one or both of us should talk to Jeremy."

Loralin picked up the phone and pushed the button that connected her to housekeeping. "Housekeeping, this is Chloe speaking." Chloe had reluctantly taken over as head of housekeeping when her predecessor had been murdered in the parking lot after the grand opening.

"Hey, it's Loralin. Could you send Jeremy Orville here to my office when he has a free moment?"

"Certainly," she agreed. "Is there anything wrong?"

Loralin kept her voice light. "No, not at all. I just want to check up on him after that disaster with Chef the other day."

"Ah, okay. He's been doing a great job for Mr. Robertson. That man is demanding, and Jeremy has been there for him whenever needed and keeps up with his other rooms, too."

"Good to hear," Loralin said. At least now she confirmed that Jeremy was indeed the housekeeper assigned to Deke's room.

* * *

Devin had gone to the kitchen to help Chef Pierre with one disaster or another, and Loralin was alone in her office when Jeremy showed up. "Chloe said you needed to see me," he said nervously.

"Yes, come on in and sit down. You're not in trouble, so you can relax."

The young man breathed a sigh of relief and did as she'd suggested. "So, why am I here then?"

Loralin looked down at the invoice on her desk and then back up at the new housekeeper. "I just wanted to make sure everything was okay after the other day, since the murder that happened a few days after you started your first shift."

For a brief moment, the young man seemed taken aback, but then he smiled at Loralin. "I'm doing fine, ma'am. Chef and I have made peace, and Mr. Robertson is a great tipper, so I've been giving him some extra attention. And don't worry, I still have plenty of time left for my other rooms."

Loralin smiled back at the newest hire. "I'm so glad to hear that. I was worried that maybe you were having trouble fitting in because of the original setbacks."

The young employee blushed just a bit. "Well, thanks, but really, I'm okay."

Loralin dismissed him and wrote a few things in the notebook. She wasn't sure what it was, but something wasn't sitting right with her. Something was going on in her hotel, and she hated not knowing exactly what it was.

* * *

Devin walked into the office and sat in front of Loralin's desk. "Crisis averted. Chef will live to cook another day, although it was iffy there for a minute. The man was having a fit because his favorite pot was in the wrong place. He actually said, 'I might as well just give up and die.'"

Loralin couldn't help but laugh. "That man is a drama queen and a half, but at least it's over for now."

"Yeah," Devin said with a sigh. "I talked with the cooks, waiters, and busboys while they were all avoiding the kitchen. According to Steven, he heard that all of the wait staff have airtight alibis. I tend to believe him, but I thought we could ask Miles just to be sure."

Loralin handed the notebook over to Devin and let him read what she'd written. "I still have no idea why Jeremy is getting so close with Deke, but something about the whole situation makes me feel uneasy."

"I think I agree," Devin said as he handed the notebook back. "There is something weird going on there. Have you heard anything from Miles about Zoey, or if he has any information on our flood guests yet?"

"No," she said with a yawn. "And I don't expect to before tomorrow. He has a lot of information to sift through. Remember, he's also hunting down Phyllis's old victims to see if any of them were in the vicinity."

"Yeah, I know," he said. He was suddenly being so morose. "We need to get this case solved as soon as possible. My dad wants me to accompany him back to Tasmania to meet the grandmother I never met."

"Oh?" Loralin said, dropping the notebook into a drawer and turning her full attention to Devin. "That... that sounds like something you should definitely do." If she thought that, then why did she feel like he was leaving her forever? Was he using it as an excuse to get away from her so he wouldn't have to make any decisions on their relationship? But he also knew she could just ask his father.

"Yeah, and I was wondering." He wiped his hands on his slacks as if he were nervous. "I was wondering if you'd come with us. I know you said you wanted to see Tasmania, and I know you didn't plan on doing it so soon. We'd have to make arrangements for the inn, but I know Maureen and Gage could handle things and..."

"Whoa," Loralin said with a laugh. Devin had a habit of talking fast and babbling when he was nervous. "Slow down. I'd love to come with you. We can start making plans whenever you're ready. I hope to have this case solved in the next couple of weeks, and if not, well, Miles just might have to do it himself."

"Okay then," Devin said with a big smile; his uneasiness from just a moment before was gone. "I'll let Dad know, and we'll go from there."

***

By one pm, Loralin was cursing the supplier that brought their cleaning supplies. They'd run low after the flood, and they had promised to have more delivered by noon that day. They were a no-show, and the housekeepers needed their supplies. "Devin, could you run into town and grab this list of supplies for me?"

"Sure thing. I'll see you at home when I'm done."

Once she was alone, Loralin locked up her office and headed out the front doors of the inn. She hadn't been to her spot on the river since the day of the flood. She figured it was time to get back out there. It was where she liked to be when she needed to think, or just decompress from the stresses of life.

The flowers all over the ground and on the banks of the river were in full bloom and so beautiful. The rain they'd gotten that day had spiraled the landscape into full spring mode.

The closer she got to the water, the louder it got. The water was still high from the flooding, and it was running fast along the riverbed. The cloudiness that had marked it the first few days after the flood was now starting to clear, and she felt peace sweep over her.

She couldn't quite tell if she was an unlucky person or if she just had two bad things happen to her in a row. First, the murder of dear sweet Penny, and then the murder of Phyllis. The small town rarely saw two murders over five years, let alone two within a few months. And two on the same property to boot.

Luck had always been one of those things that she tried not to think about much. She'd figured that if she didn't think about it, it wouldn't turn on her. But before the grand opening of the inn and the first murder, she'd had a stretch of luck she couldn't believe. She'd finally had the money to renovate the inn and reopen it as she'd promised her grandparents, and the work on the inn got done in record time, so she was able to start living her dream a whole six months earlier than she'd originally planned. And then to top it off, her original manager had eloped with a rich widow, and that's how she'd been able to convince her long-distance best friend to come live with her and help her run the inn. It had been the icing on the cake. The one thing she'd wanted more than the inn was to be able to see and spend time with Devin in person.

By the time the first murder had happened, she'd been the luckiest woman on the planet. So why were so many annoyingly bad things happening to her now? Two murders, new feelings for her roommate that she was too scared to explore, just in case she was wrong about his return feelings, and, of course, the fact that Deke Robertson might be scheming to run her out of business. The trip to Tasmania with Devin had to be her return to good luck. Otherwise, knowing the luck she'd had recently, she might just end up dying in a plane crash.

With a broken laugh, she shook the thoughts from her head. She was getting way too hooked on this whole idea of luck. One day at a time needed to be how she lived her life. And at least if she died in a plane crash, Devin would be by her side.

"Hey," came a voice from behind her. A voice she could listen to all day.

"Hey," she shot back. "How did it go in town?"

"I bought out most of the grocery store's cleaning aisle, but we are stocked now. How come you're down here?"

"I was just thinking and looking at how beautiful spring has become." She smiled at him as he moved up behind her to rest his hands on her shoulders.

"You sure? There's nothing wrong?"

"Nope. I'm all good. Let's head home and figure out what's for dinner."

"I grabbed us food from Mabel's in town. I'm just too worn out to cook."

"Oh, thank you! I didn't feel like cooking either." Loralin grabbed his hand and pulled him along the path to the cottage they shared. It was going to be a good night, bad luck be damned.

11

The Three Musketeers Go To The City

Loralin woke up in her bed alone. Devin had opted out of watching a movie that night and had gone straight to his room after dinner. Loralin had stayed up looking over the files and did some research on her computer. And that was why she hurried out of bed and into the shower. She needed to go to Casper that day. She hoped Devin would want to go with her, but if he didn't, she'd ask Heather.

Once she was dressed and ready to go, she knocked on Devin's door and waited for an answer. When she didn't get one, she opened it and looked inside. His bed was made, and he was gone.

As Loralin walked down the path that led from her home to the inn, she called Devin's cell phone.

"Hello," he answered.

"Hey, where are you?" She pretty much figured he was already at work, but he could have gone to town, too.

"I'm in your office waiting for you. I need to order some more key cards. We have several that have seen better days."

"But we've only been open a few months. What the hell are

people doing to them?" She much preferred the days when they used keys. First, keys were metal and not plastic, and they lasted for years unless they got lost. And getting a new key cut was no more than five bucks. Getting new key cards was twenty dollars each.

"I don't know. What are you going to be working on today?" The last place Devin wanted to be was work. He was getting spring fever or something. He couldn't wait to go to Tasmania with his dad and brother. And he couldn't wait to show it to Loralin. Sitting around in the office all day seemed counterproductive to getting the murders solved.

"I'm going to Casper. Want to come with me?" Loralin's tone almost sounded like she was begging him.

"Yes!" Now that was more like it. Unless, of course, they were going for inn business. Maybe they were going to the travel agents to get the tickets? Nah, it was too soon for that. "So, why are we going?"

"Well, I did some research last night when I couldn't sleep and found out that three of the five families that Phyllis destroyed still live in or around Casper. Then we have Zoey, who is still missing. And the other one that isn't accounted for moved to Montana or something."

Devin's excitement tripled. "Hell yeah, let's get on with this investigation. When will you be here?"

"Right now," she said as she opened the door and smiled at her inn's manager, and ended their call. "Ready to go?"

"Where are you going, Mama?" Heather came up behind her mother as Devin agreed he was ready. They both stepped into the office.

Loralin explained where they were going, and Heather got excited. "Do you think I could come with you? I remembered last night about one of my colleagues saying something along the lines of 'why didn't somebody kill her already' when Phyllis's promotion was announced. At the time, I didn't register who it was, but once I thought about it, it was our only male labor and delivery nurse."

"I don't see why not," her mother answered. "We might as well question everyone while we're there."

* * *

As Loralin drove, Devin and Heather strategized as to how they would approach everyone. The co-worker was easy; Heather would just talk to him casually about Phyllis's death. But the families of her victims were another story. They would have to be careful what they said.

"Maybe one of us could say we were working for the police to notify everyone about Phyllis's death." Even as she said it, Loralin knew it wasn't the way to go.

"How about we say I'm a reporter for some paper in Northern Wyoming and I'm doing a story on Phyllis's death and the destruction she caused in her job as a nurse," Devin suggested.

"I like that idea." Heather agreed with Loralin. "But what do the rest of us do while you're talking to these people one at a time?" Loralin, for one, didn't want to sit in a car waiting for him all day.

"Well," Heather started, "how about you say you guys are working together on the story? You can just drop me off at the hospital and leave me. That will give me time to talk to everyone."

"Okay then, " Devin said with a smile. "I guess we know how

we're going to do this. Now let's just hope that we get some good information."

The trip to Casper usually took only thirty minutes, but because of the detours caused by the floods, it took them closer to forty-five. In any case, they were sitting in the parking lot of Natrona County Medical Center by nine a.m.

"Alright, kiddo. Call me and let me know when you're done, and we will wrap things up and come get you," Loralin said, squeezing her daughter's hand. Heather got out of the car, and Loralin pulled away from the curb. "Where should we start?"

Devin looked at the list and read the details about the first person. Jackson Monterro had lost his wife and daughter fifteen years ago because of Phyllis. "He works at the office building out past the car dealerships on Second Street."

"Okay then," Loralin said, heading the car in the right direction. "That's where we will start."

* * *

Jackson Monterro managed a company that sold top-of-the-line office machines to companies all over Wyoming. Devin was a little worried that he might not talk to them if he was too busy, but when they walked in, only a receptionist sat at the desk. "Can I help you?" she asked with a polite smile.

"Hello, I wonder if we could speak with Mr. Monterro." Loralin had luckily dressed professionally for the trip.

"May I tell him what it's about?" the receptionist asked, reaching for the phone.

"Well, it's actually a personal matter from fifteen years ago." Devin didn't want to give away too much, so he figured he'd stick to the basics.

"Wait here, please." The receptionist hung up the phone, stood, and walked into the office behind her. When she came back out, she motioned the two to enter. "You're here about Matilda and Josie?" he asked, giving them the once-over.

"In a way," Loralin said. "We are reporters from the Gillette Gazette, and we'd like to talk to you about what happened to you fifteen years ago."

The man was shaking his head. "But why? My wife and daughter died, what does that have to do with anything now?"

Devin motioned to a seat, and the man nodded his consent that they sit. "I'm not sure if you heard, but Phyllis Palmer was murdered just over a week ago at the Robbins Nest Inn in Elk River."

Mr. Monterro's eyes widened, and he cleared his throat. "Well, I'll be damned. I never thought I'd hear that name again. I never ever wanted to, but under these circumstances, I don't mind. This is great news!"

"Is there any way we could get you to tell us your side of the story? We want to make sure everyone knows the devastation this woman caused."

Jackson Monterro leaned back in his chair. "Well, there isn't much to tell that isn't public knowledge. The monitors they used on my wife while she was in labor had malfunctioned. The nurse, Phyllis, had determined that and was supposed to replace it, but she never did. Two hours later, my wife went into convulsions and..." He took a deep breath to steady himself before continuing. "My wife and baby girl both died. Apparently. My wife's blood pressure spiked, causing a stroke of sorts, and that dropped the baby's heart rate, and before they figured out what was wrong, it was too late."

"I'm so sorry," Loralin said softly. "Did you ever find out why Phyllis hadn't changed out the monitors?"

"She didn't read my wife's chart properly about her issues with high blood pressure. If she had, she wouldn't have waited so long to change out the monitors. She just didn't do her job in any way on that day."

Devin waited a moment to let the words sink in and then disappear into the air before he spoke again. "Have the police questioned you yet? I know that when I talked to them, they were listing everyone who had filed suits against Phyllis as potential suspects."

Jackson barked out a laugh. "They haven't contacted me as yet. But I'll tell you what I'm going to tell them. As much as I would like to say that it was me, it couldn't have been. My wife Amelia, who is also my receptionist, and I were on Vacation in Vegas visiting her family. We have about forty witnesses from the family reunion."

Loralin smiled at the man, and he returned it. "I'm glad to hear that. I would hate to think of you having to deal with an investigation on top of everything that's already happened to you."

Devin and Loralin stood and thanked Jackson Monterro for his time and then walked out of the building. They remained quiet on the way to the car, each contemplating the incompetence of Phyllis Palmer.

Heather and all of her other colleagues were lucky it hadn't gotten them in trouble at some point. Although Loralin had the sneaking suspicion that eventually Phyllis would have blamed something on Heather. Just like the man they'd talked to, she thanked the heavens that Phyllis Palmer was gone.

* * *

Devin and Loralin repeated the same story with all of the others they'd come to investigate. Everyone but the parents of one of the boys who died had rock-solid alibis. They had actually been one of the rescues brought to the inn. But to Loralin's dismay, they had no record of them. One of her crew had some explaining to do. During the time of the murder, they said they had been sleeping in room 316.

"We've got to let Miles know right away," Loralin said. "He's going to flip his lid when we tell him about this couple that we didn't document."

Devin just mumbled his agreement. "I think I'm more worried about whether they recognized us. Don't you think they would have?"

All Loralin could do was shrug. "I don't know. We were both handing out room assignments, but so were three other desk clerks. Let's just hope that they wouldn't make a run for it if they did recognize us. I think Miles would arrest us both for interfering in an investigation."

Devin laughed. "He better not, or I'll tell the chief he's the one who asked us to interfere."

* * *

Just as Loralin started up her SUV, Heather called, asking to be picked up. It only took them ten minutes to get back to the hospital, and then they headed for a local family restaurant to discuss their findings over lunch.

"So," Heather said on their way to eat. "Would it be okay if I stayed with you for a while, Mama? I'll work at the hotel for you to make some money."

Loralin pulled into the restaurant parking lot and turned to look at her daughter. "Why? You're going back to your job at the hospital soon."

A blush colored Heather's face. "Well, Mama, actually, I quit my job while I was there. I want to take a break for a couple of months and then find a new nursing job somewhere closer to home."

"Wow," Loralin whispered. "Yeah, sweetheart. Your dad and I would love to have you here for a while. I just never expected this. What happened?"

"I just realized that I don't want to work for a hospital that messed up so badly in hiring and promoting Phyllis. And I sure as hell don't want to work for Tanner Healthcare anymore."

"Good enough for me," Loralin said with a smile. "My girl is so smart. Now let's go eat."

While they waited for a table, Loralin called to check on the inn. She was done by the time they took their seats. "Okay, kiddo, tell us what you found out talking to your former co-workers.

"Well," she started. "It turns out that Jeff was on his way to Elk River to attend the promotion celebration when the flood hit. He was on the Casper side of the washed-out road, so he turned around and went back home. Everyone available was called in, so he was at the hospital working when Phyllis was murdered."

Which means," Devin offered, "that all of your colleagues in Labor and Delivery were either at the inn with you or working at the hospital the morning she was killed."

"Exactly," Heather said as she handed the waiter her menu.

"Well, what happened to that new nurse who roomed with

you and Phyllis?" Loralin asked. "Why wasn't she ever a suspect?"

Heather took a drink of her iced tea. "She left right after me and was in the dining room talking to the waiter at the time of death."

Devin motioned for the waiter to come to refill his soda. "Well, at least we have a couple of possibilities out of all of the patient families that would have had it in for Phyllis. Now we just have to see if Miles came up with anything about the people who sheltered at the inn."

"Yeah," Loralin agreed. "I think I'll call him and invite him to dinner at the inn tonight. We can compare notes."

"Good Idea," Devin said, accepting a new soda. "And tell him to bring a list of everyone's alibis, I'm curious to know. Maybe we can poke holes in some of them."

"I hope we don't get too many suspects," Loralin said with a chuckle. "Although we don't want to get too few either. I just hope that something will now lead to a prime suspect and we can get this over with." She had been helping Miles solve mysteries long enough to know that her gut was telling her that they were missing something. And her gut was never wrong. Unless the stress of a second murder and her relationship with Devin was throwing her off. In either case, she didn't know what to think.

* * *

Loralin and Devin stopped by the cottage to freshen up before heading to the inn to meet Miles. She'd been thinking a lot about the trip to Tasmania. "Hey Dev, do you think we could take the whole family to Australia? We'd let you and your dad have your time with your grandmother, but I think it would be nice if the girls and Matthew could come too."

Devin was standing behind her, and when she turned around, he smiled and wrapped her in his arms. "I had the same thought. I just hadn't told you about it yet."

Lorlin smiled back at him. "You really have become a hugger, haven't you?"

"I guess I have." He leaned in and pressed his lips to hers. "I'm thinking about becoming a kisser too. I have to say you're the best kisser I've ever encountered."

"Really," she grinned ear to ear. "Thank you." Coming from Devin, it meant the world to her. She knew she was a good kisser, but sometimes she felt inadequate compared to all of the younger women Devin had in his past.

"So, is there anything else I'm the best at?" she asked. She had to look away from him. She didn't know what had made her say that. She wasn't the type to beg for validation about her sex life.

"Loralin, I have to say that…" His phone rang, and he pulled away to look at it.

She knew the burst of intimacy that could have answered all their questions about their relationship was over now. This was the time of day his mom called him.

"Hey Mom, is everything okay?" Devin's eyes clouded over. "Yes, we are going to Tasmania soon, Ma. Dad has to go see his mother."

Everything was quiet, and Loralin excused herself. "I'll meet you at the inn," she whispered.

* * *

Miles and Loralin were just sitting down to dinner at the owner's table when Devin showed up. "How's your mum?" she asked.

"She's hanging in there," Devin said with a sigh. "She's upset that we are visiting Tasmania and she can't."

"I'm sorry," Loralin said, reaching over to touch his upper arm. She regretted it immediately because he pulled away, and it made her heart hurt. Until he came to terms with his issues with his mother, there was no way they could be anything but friends. She didn't even know which way to turn, but she wouldn't be able to make that decision until she knew what he was capable of reciprocating.

Head Waiter Steven brought the drinks that Miles had ordered for everyone and took their food orders, then left them to talk. Loralin started by telling Miles about the couple that had been there in the flood, but never officially checked in. He didn't seem too happy, but he didn't freak out either.

"So, do you have their names?" Miles asked. "I'll be questioning them tomorrow in Casper.

"Yeah, Loralin said, pulling out her notes. Joseph and Mariline Franco. Their baby boy died of pneumonia after Phyllis didn't suck the poop-polluted fluid out of his lungs. By the time the pediatrician did, it was too late."

"Okay," Miles said with a sigh. "That woman…" He laughed. "I was going to say she should have been shot, but I guess strangled is close enough."

Devin and Loralin chuckled along with him. "So, I guess that's it. We have the Francos, Zoey, and Hank as suspects worth looking into. Did you find anything on the flood shelter guests?"

"There was one man who had worked with Phyllis many

years ago. I found out he was in the medical field and did a search. When I contacted him, he told me that he and his wife were in the dining room and then the lobby from 5 a.m. until they left at 2 p.m. I just have to find people who remember them being there."

"Okay," Loralin said, pushing her plate away. "Do you want us to do that?"

"No," Miles said. "The chief is on my ass to do more, even though he's assigning us other stuff. I'll take care of questioning your staff. But I think you should just lie low for a few days. And then we can regroup and see what we've got."

"Sounds good to me," Devin said. "Tomorrow is my day off, and I'm going fishing with my dad and my brother. It will be nice to forget about this horrid case for a few days."

"And I have plans with the river tomorrow," Loralin said. "I need to just go there and think. Maybe I'll take my work down there and see what I can get done."

12

Bread & Milk

It had been decided that Heather would stay with her father while she was taking her sabbatical. That way, Devin wouldn't be put out by losing his room. When Loralin woke up the next morning, her house wasn't as quiet as it usually was. She could hear Devin and his family being entertained by Hanna. Her daughter was undoubtedly telling them some embarrassing story about her childhood that Loralin was involved in.

"Good Morning, everyone," Loralin said as she walked into the living room wearing a pair of shorts and a tank top. For a woman who was heading up in years, her legs were still trim and smooth, and her arms had yet to show any wrinkly skin. "I thought you gentlemen were going fishing."

"We are," Devin said. "We were just trying to figure out where to go."

"And then," Hanna slipped in. "I told them about the time we went fishing on the Elk River at Johnson's Point in Boone."

Loralin groaned and smacked her head. "Please tell me you didn't tell them about how I stood up and tipped the boat over because a fish jumped in and scared me when it landed in my lap."

"That's exactly what I told them, Mama," Hanna said, her voice filled with laughter. "And now they want me to show them the place."

"Well, good," she said, glaring playfully, "You guys can go to Johnson's Point and leave me to my peaceful day by the river."

That was their cue to leave, and within minutes, Loralin was alone in the house. She'd made a picnic lunch the night before when they'd arrived home, and she had several file folders worth of work in her bag along with her laptop. All she had to do was grab some breakfast, and then she could take off, too. Her favorite place on the river awaited her. And it wasn't the spot that many people thought was her favorite. Even Devin didn't know this spot.

The place she was headed to was about a ten-minute walk in the opposite direction from her one spot. It was off behind her house, where the river curved around and was no longer parallel to the Inn. About two minutes into her trek, she felt a little uneasy, like she was being watched. Stopping, she set the picnic basket down and turned slowly in all directions to see if she could spot something that would make her feel like that. When she didn't, she reached into the picnic basket and took out her pistol, attaching it to her hip.

Springtime was one of the most dangerous times for wild animals in the area, and she didn't want to be caught unawares. But on second thought, she knew her pistol wouldn't work on the bigger wild animals, so she turned around and headed back to the cottage to get her rifle out of the gun safe in the spare bedroom.

Once she was back on the trail, she could feel the stress fade away, and her body relax. The place she was going had soft grasses and flowers on the bank, whereas most places just had rocks, twigs, and spotty patches of grass. In this place, she could spread out her picnic blanket and enjoy the noise of the rushing water, the chirping birds, and the wind in the trees on the opposite bank.

When the water had flooded the bank, it hadn't trampled down the vegetation as she had feared. Everything was pristine, and the only sign that there had been water over the banks was that the grass was even greener than normal and the flowers seemed to have multiplied by ten. Spreading the blanket out as close to the river as she dared get, she took a seat and closed her eyes. She let the sun beat down on her face and breathed in the fragrant air. She already felt a hundred times better.

Once the sun had warmed her thoroughly, she grabbed her bag and took out her laptop. She was happy she'd invested in a sunshade for it, or she wouldn't have been able to read anything on it. What most people didn't know was that when she took a day off like this, to be alone, she usually sat in this very spot and wrote. She knew she would never publish anything, but she loved the idea of writing a mystery novel. So, many years before, she'd started one, and this had seemed like the perfect time to work on it. Of course, she would also do a few handwritten invoices that she'd included in her bag so she wouldn't technically be lying about why she'd taken this time off.

* * *

The story had just been flowing out of her, and when she checked, she'd written seven thousand words. She wasn't sure why it flowed so well now, but she wouldn't dwell on it. She was at a point where she needed to do some research, so she put it away and decided to eat the lunch she'd packed.

Just as she took the first bite of her sandwich, she heard a noise from behind her. When she turned to look, she didn't see a person or an animal, but she did see something floating down the river. Standing up, she waded into the water, which only reached her knees at that point in the river. A bread wrapper and a half-gallon milk jug were coming right at her.

Wading in a bit further, she was able to grab it and pull it out of the water to be disposed of along with her own trash. Then she heard another noise in the trees. "Hello!" she hollered. "Is there someone there? Would you like to join me for lunch?"

When her echo had faded, she didn't hear any more noise coming from the trees, or anywhere for that matter. The birds had quieted, and the breeze hadn't been blowing right then. "That's strange," she mumbled to herself. "There had to have been someone out there, or the birds would still be chirping, and there wouldn't have been trash floating down the river.

Overnight camping and fishing weren't allowed on this part of the river, so there shouldn't have been anything more than a hiker or a picnicker around. But a whole loaf of bread and a whole half gallon of milk didn't seem like something you'd bring for a few hours on the river.

Her favorite place seemed to lose some of its peace now that someone else was there. After lunch, she'd head back home and finish her work in her kitchen, where she could truly be alone.

Instead of walking her usual route, through the meadow, she decided to walk home along the bank and see if she could see anything out of place. It would take her about twenty minutes, but the day was beautiful, not too hot and not too cool, so the exercise would do her good.

When she was about ten minutes from home, Loralin found what looked like some used charcoal bricks on the bank. When she walked over and moved her hand toward them, she realized they were wet and cold. They could have washed up from anywhere. It was against the law to bring grills into the area, but many people still did. She would tell Miles and see if the department could send someone to check it out. The last thing she needed was to have a brush fire take out her cottage and her inn in one fell swoop.

* * *

As soon as Loralin reached the cottage, she put her stuff away and sat down at the table to do the last two handwritten invoices, one of which was to the hospital for their promotion celebration party. Once her work was done, she figured she would try to work out what to do for dinner. But just as she texted Devin to see if he had a preference, the noisy bunch came through the front door. "Hey, did you guys have fun?"

"Yeah," Trevor said, his eyes bright with excitement and his face pink from the summer sun. "And Hanna didn't stand up and knock us over when I caught a fish and accidentally swung it in her face."

Loralin laughed and looked at her daughter. "I guess you don't scare as much as I do."

"Truthfully, I was too scared to move," she said with a blush on her cheeks.

"Did you have fun?" Devin asked.

"Not really," Loralin said. "Well, I mean, I did, but some

strange stuff happened.

"Want to tell me about it?" he finally asked when she stopped speaking.

"Not right now. I don't want to scare small ears," she said, pointing to Trevor, who was helping Hanna put their stuff away.

"Okay," Devin agreed. "We'll talk after they leave."

Loralin could tell that he was worried, and she felt bad. She would have to reassure him, but first, she had to help clean and freeze their catches.

"It was a great day for fishing," Mark said as he handed her a knife. "They were biting like crazy where we were. The other folks we met there said they had been down here just past the inn, and the fish weren't biting. They didn't even stay an hour. Probably figured it was because of all the trash they found on the bank."

"Where exactly? Did they say?" Loralin asked.

"Moss corners or something like that," Mark told her. "They said the fish almost seemed spooked and were swimming the other way."

Moss Corners was near where Loralin had been. There had to be something going on there. She needed to call Miles as soon as possible.

* * *

The men went out onto the back patio, and Hanna was in the kitchen calling her sister to see if she wanted to join them for dinner. Loralin stepped into her room and called Miles. "This is Miles," he answered.

"Hey, I've got some information for you."

"Okay..." He hesitated for just a moment. "What do you have?"

Loralin told him about her feelings of being watched, hearing rustling in the woods, and the trash in the river. Then she told him about the fishing spot just up the road that wasn't yielding any fish.

"That's interesting," Miles murmured. "Are you thinking what I'm thinking?"

Loralin nodded even though she knew he couldn't see her. "Zoey and Hank are hiding in the woods."

"Yep. I'm going to head out to your place to question everyone, and then we'll try to start a search at first light."

"Okay. If you want, bring Meredith and Gabe. We're going to have a barbecue."

"Sounds good," he said. "We'll be there in about twenty minutes."

* * *

Dinner was on by the time Heather, Miles, his wife, and stepson showed up. The entire group sat outside in the beautiful Wyoming spring evening, enjoying good food and good company. But as the sun started to fade and the mosquitoes came out, everyone moved inside, where the two kids settled into Devin's room in front of his gaming console, and the adults gathered around the dining room table to discuss the missing murder suspects.

He started by questioning Hanna, Devin, and Mark about what they'd heard while they were fishing. "Loralin, do you still have the trash you fished out of the river?"

"Um... yeah, why? It's in my picnic basket." She wondered

why he was so interested in empty packaging.

"Could you grab it for me?"

Devin stood. "I'll get it. It's easier for me to get out." When he brought it back, Miles had fetched a large plastic zipper bag and had Devin put the bread wrapper in it. He used a plastic grocery bag to put the milk carton in.

"Why are you bagging them?" Loralin asked. "Wouldn't prints be washed off?"

"There was some stuff stolen from Grady's Grocery the other day, a loaf of this kind of bread, a half-gallon of this kind of milk, and a jar of peanut butter. I think it's best if we keep this safe in case we need to make a case."

Now Loralin understood, and she nodded her head in agreement. "So, has the search party been organized?"

Miles barked out a laugh. "I'm still waiting to hear from Morris to see if he'll allow it. If he doesn't, concerned citizens might do it themselves."

When Miles's phone rang, he got up and left the table. They heard him arguing with his boss, and then he came back. "Well, I got a search party, but the Chief isn't too excited about it. And I can only use five men, other than myself."

"Will that be enough?" Mark asked.

"I hope so," Miles returned. "But I wouldn't be opposed if a civilian or two paired with each officer."

Devin and Mark both nodded their understanding. They would be helping the Elk River PD search for Zoey and Hank first thing in the morning. And both Loralin and Devin knew they would be turning in early without a movie-watching marathon because the day would start at 5 a.m. They would all meet at the inn and go from there.

* * *

"Good Morning," Loralin said with a yawn as she filled the large coffee dispenser that she'd brought to the lobby for the search party. There was plenty of it, and it was hot.

"Morning," Miles returned. "I want you, Heather, and Hanna to stay here and man the phones and walkie-talkies. And if you hear the SOS signal, call the chief and send in the cavalry."

"Yes, sir," Hanna said, saluting her dad. "Don't worry, we've got it all under control."

"Alright," Miles hollered. "We all have our assignments. If there are any questions, ask now. Otherwise, let's get going!"

When the door opened, and the men poured out, the people inside heard the echo of a couple of hound dogs. "What on earth?" Loralin said, stepping outside.

"Jim Murray offered the use of his dogs," Sargent Henderson said as she took control of one of them. "He's not employed directly by the police department, so he can volunteer the use of his dogs for any reason."

Loralin laughed and turned back inside. "I wonder if the Chief is mad about that. This search party that he didn't want was now bolstered by the two best bloodhounds in the state. No wonder Chief Morris wanted out. It seemed he was losing respect left and right.

Hanna and Heather laughed too. "I just hope they find them. Do you think they did it?" Heather asked.

"I don't know," Loralin said quietly. "I guess we'll soon find out."

Twenty minutes later, you could hear the bloodhounds baying and men shouting, even from the inn. Radio chatter had let the women know that they had found some kind of campsite, not far from where Loralin had been the day before.

"Loralin," came Mile's voice over the walkie-talkie.

"Yes, Miles, is everything okay?" She couldn't tell from his voice because of the static over the line.

"They must have moved on from this site sometime early yesterday. We are bagging everything we found here, and then we're moving upstream. "If you have to start work soon, just make sure someone else is briefed and knows what to do."

"I'll be here," she said. "The inn is in good hands." There was no way she'd miss this manhunt. She's the one who found the items that led them to believe the pair was nearby. She would follow it through until the end. Even if it took all day.

But Loralin did leave the communications station set up by the police in the lobby. They hadn't wrapped things up as quickly as they'd wanted, so Loralin and Chef were going to bring lunch to the troops at her house. They would get a quick meal on her back patio and then go back to looking. The hunt would end at dark if they hadn't found them by then.

"How's it going?" Loralin asked Devin as they sat side by side, eating one of Chef's famous hoagies.

"Good. I think they've been moving every day or so. We've found a few more old campsites, but we are thinking they may have changed sides of the river."

"How much longer will the dogs be able to work?" Chef asked the young man.

"They will be good for the rest of the day. I just hope that these yahoos haven't moved out of the area. They may have seen Loralin yesterday and taken off.

Miles stood up and called for attention to brief the men. "Alright, you've been refreshed and used the facilities. Let's get back out there!"

Before they could leave, however, the two hounds started howling and nearly yanked Sargent Henderson, who was taking care of them during the break, off her feet.

The dog's trainer ran over and took hold of one of the dogs, and Henderson kept the other. And they were all off and running away from the river. "Where are they going?" Miles Hollered. "Loralin, is that old workshop of your grandfather's still standing?"

"I don't know for sure. I think it was half blown down last time I was there!"

As the police and civilian search party headed off in the direction the dogs led, Loralin sent the chef back to the inn and took off after Devin and Miles.

"You should go home," Devin said as she jogged beside him.

"I'll pretend you didn't say that," she huffed as she kept pace with him. "If those two are hiding on my property, I need to be there when they are caught."

Suddenly, the officers in front of them and the two dogs came to a stop about fifteen feet from her grandfather's old workshop. She'd been right, half of the roof was caved in, but the other half was fine.

"Zoey, Hank, come out with your hands up!" Miles yelled through the megaphone he held. "Come on out now!"

There was silence and then rustling in the distance.

"Come on now! Don't make us come in there and get you." Miles stepped to the front of the group.

After just a few seconds, the door of the old shop creaked open, and Hank stepped out with his hands up. Zoey was right behind him. "We... we didn't do anything," she whined. "We were just camping."

Not a few seconds later, officers had the two on the ground, and they were cuffed. Loralin turned toward home then. They were in custody, and her property was safe again. Now she needed to get back to the inn and get on with her work.

* * *

Loralin was just finishing up cleaning a couple of rooms when Devin made it back to the inn. She'd let Lisa Marie head home earlier when she'd complained of a migraine and an upset stomach. These were the days she liked. Being hands-on with the day-to-day operation of the inn sometimes was nice. It made her feel like she was there to do more than push papers and order supplies.

"Hey," Devin said when he saw Loralin heading into her office.

"Oh, hey! How did the arrest go?" A big part of her was curious about what was going on with the couple they'd found on her property, but for some reason, another part of her wanted to just be done with it all.

"They are denying ever killing Phyllis," he told her. "But they have no solid alibi for that morning. Apparently, they'd been sleeping in their truck's camper shell in the parking lot."

"What? Really? How did I miss that?" She knew exactly how, though. She or Devin used to make several daily rounds around the property, including the parking lot. But recently, after the first murder had been solved, they'd let it slide. "What time did they clock in that day?"

"Eight-thirty," he answered as he sat and leaned back in the chair. "They insisted that some people had seen them in the truck, but they hadn't been able to find anyone."

"So, what's going to happen now?" she asked as she too

leaned back in her chair and looked at her best Devin.

"I don't know. Miles says they have enough trespassing and illegal camping charges to keep them in jail while the murder is investigated. But as far as he and the Chief are concerned, they have their murderers."

"And what do you think?" she asked her fellow sleuth.

"I think I agree. They had motive and opportunity. We just need some of that forensic evidence to link to them, and it will be practically open and shut."

"Yeah. I wish there had been an eyewitness or something. That would be even better." Loralin wanted the case to be over, but she also wanted to make sure the right people were punished. She was kicking herself for not staying to witness what happened after they exited the building. It may have given her a sense of whether they were guilty or not. But for now, she had to rely on what Miles and Devin told her.

A knock on the door interrupted the couple's contemplative moment. "Come in," Loralin hollered.

"Ma'am," Jeromy said softly as he stepped into the room.

"Go ahead and shut the door, man. Come on in." Devin got up and motioned for the young man to take his seat.

"Uh... thanks. I uh, I heard about the couple that worked here being arrested. I don't know if this is important, but I did see the two of them arguing with the dead lady in the dining room after dinner the night before the murder."

Loralin smiled at the nervous young man and picked up her phone. "Miles, it's Loralin. Call me back when you can. One of our housekeepers witnessed an exchange between Zoey, Hank, and Phyllis the night before the murder."

Devin, who had moved over to one of the filing cabinets, came back and sat in the chair next to Jeromy. "This information might be useful to the police. It was good you came forward."

"Great," the young man said softly. "I didn't want to get into trouble for not saying something about it earlier, but once they were arrested, I figured it was my duty."

"Well," Loralin said. "The police know now. I'm sure Detective Robbins will stop by to question you."

"That's fine, Ma'am." He stood and motioned to the door. "I'm going to head back to work. Thanks."

Devin stood and walked him out, then returned to Loralin. "It seems our murderous couple confronted Phyllis. Unless they were defending themselves against an attack by her about their cleaning abilities."

Loralin chuckled. "Jeremy was assigned to their room, so I doubt it was that. Phyllis must have been pissed beyond words. I wonder if Heather or that new nurse would be able to tell Miles what her state of mind was after dinner that night."

Another knock sounded on the door, and Miles wandered in before she could answer. "I got your message. Would it be possible to question that housekeeper now?"

* * *

Loralin and Devin were just about to head home for dinner when Miles stopped into the office again. He'd questioned both Jeremy and Heather. "It seems that Phyllis was fit to be tied when she returned to the room. She was saying stuff about being misunderstood and hating being threatened about stuff that was someone else's fault."

"Well, it's not concrete evidence, but it will add to the whole picture. Any idea when the forensics will be back?" Loralin knew how long the forensics could take now that Elk River had lost its team. Pretty much every small town had to deal with the state lab now, and it was backed up.

"I'm hoping for no more than another week," Miles told them. "But who knows? I'll be able to keep these yahoos in jail for quite a while just based on these other charges. They are ready to plead guilty to them. They still insist that they didn't kill Phyllis, though."

"Well then," Devin said. "They'd better hope that someone comes forward saying they saw them in the parking lot, sleeping in their truck."

When Miles left, they gathered their stuff and headed back to the cottage, where they planned to start making arrangements for the trip to Australia.

It didn't take long for them to pick dates, buy tickets, and make sure everyone's passports and visas were up to date. So by the time Loralin was yawning and could barely keep her eyes open, the trip was set. "Not long from now, you get to show me where little Devin grew up."

Devin rolled his eyes and tried to hide a grin. "I can also show you where grown-up Devin did a few things, too. Like the hotel my parents used to own, the place where I lost my virginity, the place where I had my first job, and the place where I first talked to you on video chat."

For some reason, all of those things he mentioned made her even more excited. She couldn't wait to feel a part of his life like he did hers. And, she'd never been to Australia, so this would be something new. "I'll hold you to that. Now go to bed. We have work in the morning."

13

Murder & Mint-Chip Ice Cream

Devin woke up with his alarm and went to find Loralin. The house was empty. Even Hanna wasn't there. Instead of hurrying to get to work and see what Loralin was doing out of bed so early, he took his time and made some toast and coffee for breakfast. Then he enjoyed a hot shower and read the morning news on his phone. It wasn't until a phone call came through from Loralin that he decided it was time to get dressed and go to work. "Hello."

"Hey, are you coming to work today?" she asked.

"Yeah, just enjoying some me time," he returned. "I'll be there soon. Is there something important going on?"

Loralin excused herself from the phone for a moment and talked to someone else. "Okay, Devin, sorry about that. We have a meeting with two housekeepers and a prep cook about things they noticed Deke doing."

"Ah. I wonder what the hell his deal is. Shouldn't he have been gone by now?"

Loralin sighed. "Yeah, but some of his business got delayed, so he booked another couple of weeks."

"Right," Devin snickered. "More like he needs more time to concoct a plan to try to take the inn."

"Probably," Loralin murmured. "But he won't succeed. I'll see you in a few, okay?"

"Yep." Devin hung up the phone and finished getting dressed before he slipped out the front door and walked to the inn. He sure loved the place. It had quickly become home to him. He knew deep down inside that anywhere Loralin was, was home. It could be there, it could be in Tasmania, it could be in the wilds of Africa; as long as he had her, he would be home. He put it out of his mind that being friends wasn't supposed to give a person feelings like that. There was more to it, and he was too scared to face it.

"Hey," Loralin said with a smile as he walked into the inn. "Everyone's already in my office. Let's go."

When Devin walked in, he saw Chloe and Stuart from housekeeping and Marcus from the kitchen. He wondered what kind of news they could have on their shifty guest. But from the looks on their faces, it seemed like it was of the utmost importance. "Hey, everyone. Who wants to go first?"

"I guess I will," Stuart said. "Last night, I was taking stuff down to the laundry room in the basement, and I stopped by the boiler room with some trash to burn. I heard Deke Robertson come out of the laundry room and say something to another man. At first, I didn't recognize them, but as they were leaving the area, I peeked out into the hall.

"Okay," Loralin encouraged. "What did you hear them say?"

"Deke called Jeremy stupid and told him he should have waited until he got there to do anything." Stuart looked at his bosses.

"Okay, that's interesting." Loralin contemplated. "Did you

notice anything out of place when you went into the laundry room?"

"No ma'am," he answered. "I checked everything, and it was business as usual."

Loralin nodded and pointed to Chloe. "What do you have to report?"

"As I was leaving last night, I heard Jeremy and Deke in the parking lot arguing. They stopped talking and moved toward the building when they saw me."

"Did you hear what they said?" Devin asked.

"It was something about Jeromy telling Deke that he couldn't force him to do something, and Deke saying like hell he couldn't."

"Interesting," Devin said quietly. "I wonder what that's all about. What about you, Marcus?"

"Well," the young man said. "I saw Jeremy sneaking out of Deke's room in the middle of the night, wearing street clothes, and he was well off shift."

Loralin was most shocked by the last revelation. Why would her housekeeper be visiting with Deke Robertson late at night? She knew he wasn't gay. He was a known ladies' man. Unless, of course, that was something he hid from everybody. "Okay, guys, thanks for all of your hard work. You can head back to your posts now."

Once they were gone, she turned to Devin. "What in the hell is going on?"

"I don't know," he murmured. "But we're going to find out. I think it's time to have Miles investigate our newest housekeeper."

"And," Loralin stated. "I'm going to do some digging on our special guest."

***

When Loralin saw Devin again, it was ten p.m., and he was just walking in the door. "Where have you been?"

"The dishwasher broke down, and one of the ovens was overheating. I had to get the repairman out so we could serve dinner, and then I stayed around to help Chef and his people clean up."

"You should have called," she reprimanded. "I would have come to help."

Devin smiled and sat down next to her. "That's okay, I figured you could use the rest."

"Why are you looking at me like that?" she asked, unable to avoid his eyes.

"Like what?" he asked innocently. "I can't smile at you anymore?"

"You are looking at me like you're about to devour me."

"Maybe I am," he whispered, leaning in close. "I think maybe…"

"Shhh…" she warned. "Don't say something you can't take back unless you are 100 percent sure."

Instead of saying anything, Devin leaned in and pressed his lips to hers. "It's not fair to either of us to keep doing this without knowing why or what will become of it." His voice was soft, but his words were strong, and he looked directly into her eyes.

"I know," she agreed, returning his gaze. "But I'd rather it be this way than to think it was more and then have it stripped away."

Devin's gaze faltered. "Do you want me to leave?"

Loralin shook her head. "Leave, leave, or just leave from this moment?" Her heart was thundering. Did he think she wanted him gone for good?

"From this moment," he answered. "You're not getting rid of me that quickly."

Loralin reached out and pulled him in for another kiss. There was nothing wrong with kissing if you were both in denial about your feelings, right? And she wanted to get all of him she could because her biggest fear at the moment was that they would go to Tasmania and he would miss home so much that he would stay. If that happened, her world would never be the same again.

* * *

"Hey, you okay? Devin asked as he situated himself under the covers, and she lay her head on his chest.

"Yeah, I'm pretty damn good," she said with a satisfied smile creeping onto her face. "You okay?"

"Never been better," he said with the same satisfied smile.

"We've never actually talked afterward," Loralin mused. "I'm not sure what young people talk about after great sex."

Devin chuckled. "Great sex, huh? And young people probably talk about the same things as you old fogies."

"Oh," Loralin said in a teasing voice. "You mean we are going to talk about which knee almost gave out, how sore our hips are, and how we should try to use a pillow to prop up the sore body part next time?"

Devin outright laughed. "Okay, so maybe not exactly the same stuff. Are you really hurting that bad?" His voice was a mixture of disbelief and concern.

Loralin groaned. "I wouldn't say that describes me right

now. At this moment, I'm more that good kind of sore from a good workout. And in the morning, I will probably feel like I overdid it just a smidge. But you know, that kind of pain isn't so bad. It makes you feel like you did something amazing and are being rewarded for it."

"Well then," Devin whispered. "Maybe we'll do it again in a bit, and you can feel double the reward."

Loralin smiled but hid her face in his chest. Honestly, she could go for that. But it seemed her phone had other ideas. It rang, and when she ignored it, it rang again.

"Hello."

"Did I wake you?" Miles asked.

Loralin sat up straight in bed. "Umm, no. Devin and I were just hanging out and chatting."

"Right," Miles said, amusement coloring his voice. "Anyway, I just wanted to let you know we are bringing in that couple that Phyllis victimized. The ones who were traveling through the area during the murder timeline."

"Oh. I thought you had Zoey and Hank on the hook for the murder." As soon as she said it, she knew the flaw in her logic. The police needed to be as thorough as possible and rule out every possible suspect. They didn't want to be accused of railroading people. "Never mind. I shouldn't have said that."

"Yeah," he agreed. "As much as I want this to be over, we need to investigate all we can. Zoey and Hank aren't admitting to anything, so maybe I can crack these people."

"Maybe. I just can't help but feel that something is all wrong with this case, but I have no idea what. Some moments I feel like Zoey and Hank had to have done it, and then another moment I feel like we are way off base."

"Same," Miles said softly. "Maybe this case is just too close to home for all of us. We all hated Phyllis and couldn't be a hundred percent impartial."

Loralin nodded even though he couldn't see her. "I know. Did you ever contemplate giving the case over to the Cheyenne Police?"

"You know the answer to that. As long as Don Peterson runs that department, I refuse to ask for their help."

Loralin rolled her eyes and wished he could see her. "You had Don's help with the last case."

"No," Miles corrected. "You had Don's help and passed the information along to me.

Fair enough. She was the one who had asked Don to help them. And he only did it because she promised him a date. It wasn't her fault that she was almost murdered right before their date, and it never happened. "Okay. Well, let us know what you find out from that couple, and we will go from there. I have a mess with Deke Robertson to worry about now at the Inn, but I'm already vested in this case, so I'll do what I can."

"Thanks, Loralin," Miles said. "Don't overdo it too much, old lady. Good night."

"You son of a…" but she didn't finish her sentence before the dial tone cut her off.

***

Loralin woke up on her stomach with Devin's legs resting on hers. He had this weird way of sleeping diagonally on the bed. "Devin, your phone."

"What? Oh, okay…" She felt his legs move off of her, and then he sat up on the edge of the bed. "This is Devin."

Loralin watched as his sleepy, just-woken-up look was

replaced by one of annoyance. Whatever it was had to do with the inn. "What?"

He raised a finger, said a few words, then hung up. "It seems that our newest housekeeper didn't show up for work. His number was out of order, and no one answered the door when Stuart went over there to check on him. He looked in the window, and the apartment was empty."

"So the little shit was up to something with Deke, and once he knew we'd caught on, he disappeared." Loralin had just about had it with Deke Robertson. She even wondered if anyone had it in for him enough to make him the next person who died at the Robbins Nest Inn.

"Don't even think about it," Devin warned. "After so many years of knowing her, he knew exactly where her mind had gone. "No more murders at this inn."

"I know, I know. I guess instead of working the mid-shift today, we should go in now and speak with our dear friend Deke." She had been looking forward to sleeping in, and she was going to blame the annoying, unethical hotelier for that, too.

"Yep. Want the bathroom first?" Devin asked as he headed to his room to get fresh clothes.

"Nope. Join me in there when you get your stuff. We need to conserve water, remember."

***

Loralin and Devin walked into the inn together and moved behind the counter. With the pressing of three buttons, the phone in Deke Robertson's room was ringing. "Hello."

"Deke, this is Loralin. I was wondering if you could come

down to my office so we could have a private conversation." She would bet a million dollars that he believed he was about to score a new property with the Robbins Nest Inn.

"I'll be there after I grab some breakfast. Give me an hour." How could one man not only look smug all the time but sound smug too?

"We'll see you then." She still wasn't sure what she'd say to him. She wasn't even sure what all of the information she had on him meant. But the one thing she had to do was make sure that he knew, without a single doubt, that she would let the inn fail or burn to the ground before she would ever sell it to him.

Loralin busied herself with paperwork while Devin worked Maureen's first break for her so she could run to town and get her daughter, and take her to the rec center for day camp. As she set a paper on her desk, she moved her phone out of the way. Had anyone called to report Jeremy Orville missing? Shouldn't someone do that? Somebody somewhere that wasn't Deke would be missing him, surely.

Picking up her phone, she dialed Miles. He answered on the first ring. "Hey Loralin, I'm headed to Cheyenne because the Chief wants us to help on a case there. Can I call you back when I get home tonight?"

"Sure," Loralin said. "I just wanted to report a missing person."

"Oh," Miles said. "I'm in the car, so I can't write anything down. Call Sargent Henderson and give her the info. Is it about Phyllis's case?"

"No," Loralin was quick to reassure him. "It's about something going on here at the inn. I'll tell you about it tonight."

"Great," Miles answered. "Meet me at my house around eight.

I'll have Meredith and the girls fix us a late dinner, and we can discuss everything that's happened today."

"Sounds good. Drive safe, Miles."

Loralin hung up the phone just as Devin walked in. "Maureen is back, and the desk is running smoothly. Deke should be here in about fifteen minutes."

"Good," Loralin said with a smile. "That gives me time to call Sargent Henderson and give her a missing person's report on Jeremy."

"Really?" Devin questioned. From the look on Loralin's face, he knew she was up to something, but he was unsure if he should ask about it. "Do I even want to know?"

"Probably, but maybe not yet."

* * *

"I just want to hit that man, right across his smug face, with a baseball bat, or a flip flop, or anything that would hurt." Loralin was fuming after Deke Robertson left her office.

"Did you really expect him to just come clean with you and admit to conspiring with our now missing housekeeper to ruin the inn enough to sweep it out from under you?" Devin tried to be a realist as much as possible.

"No," Loralin admitted with a sigh. "But I did expect to get something out of him. He is just so smug and full of himself."

"He is. But I think cracking him is going to take time." Devin also knew a lot about smug assholes. His mother was one of the biggest Loralin had ever met.

"Yeah, I guess," she reluctantly admitted. "I think I'm going to head home and call Jackson Fairway and make sure everything is on the up and up with all of the inn's legal issues. I don't want to take the chance that Deke just decides to forgo sabotage and go for some legal loophole." There were two things in this world she couldn't lose: The Robbin's Nest Inn and Devin.

"Okay, you do that. I'll hold the fort down here." Devin hated to have her so worked up over something that was probably nothing, but he had to let her do her thing, or she wouldn't feel better.

* * *

It was half past seven when Devin headed home to get Loralin so they could go to dinner at Miles's. She was waiting for him in the carport. "So, what exactly is this dinner about?" he asked.

"Miles wants to let us know what happened with that couple that we found in Casper." Loralin handed him her keys so he could drive them. She wasn't feeling much like doing anything at the moment.

"I wonder if they've been ruled out." He knew they still didn't have forensic results yet. All he knew was that this case had to go away soon. All he could think about was taking Loralin to see his hometown. He wasn't sure why, but ever since they had been sleeping together, it was all he could think about.

"I don't know. I just want this to be over." She wanted it all to be over. It was weird how she'd only owned the inn for a few months, and she already needed a vacation. But she guessed that's what happened when you had to deal with two on-site murders, a grand opening, a new relationship, or whatever it was, and fighting to keep the place running despite the murders.

Devin knew exactly where she was coming from. "Any news

on our missing housekeeper? I'm really hoping he's not dead on the property or something."

Loralin groaned and let her head rest against the side window. "I never thought of that possibility. I sure as hell hope he's far away from here because then at least he'd be alive and we wouldn't have one more PR nightmare to deal with."

"Sorry," he mumbled. He needed to keep his big mouth shut. The last thing she needed now was more stress.

"It's okay," she said with a small smile. "Sargent Henderson took the report and said they would look into it. She's going to stop by tonight to pick up Jeremy Orville's file from Gage."

"Well, good," Devin said. At least something was moving forward, even if it wasn't the murder investigation or conviction.

Neither of them talked for the rest of the ride to Miles's house. The mood for both was somber, and for some reason, they just couldn't shake it. Hopefully, the news Miles had for them could do it.

"Welcome!" Meredith gushed when she opened the door to them. "Gabe, the girls, and I have already eaten, so you and Miles can talk business all you want. "He's in the dining room."

"Thank you," Loralin returned. "Something smells delicious."

"Pot roast and mashed potatoes with veggies," she told them before turning toward the family room. Loralin and Devin headed straight for the dining room, where Miles was looking through a file folder. Three plates of fragrant food waited for them in their usual spots around the table.

Once they were seated and eating, Miles looked at them, his expression serious. "So, that couple you told me about," he started. "It appears most of what they told you was the truth. But what they neglected to tell you, because they recognized you, was that they weren't asleep at the time of the murder, but in fact, Mrs. Franco was in their room with a swollen ankle from tripping over the bath mat, and Mr. Franco was wandering the third-floor hallway looking for an ice machine."

"But we don't have ice machines in the hallways yet," Loralin stated. "The flier right by the phone says to call the kitchen for ice."

"I know," Miles said. "Mr. Franco says he wandered the third floor and then decided to go to the kitchen and ask. By the time he got back to his room, forty-five minutes later, Mrs. Franco was asleep."

"So," Devin asked. "What you're saying is that Mrs. Franco could have faked the injury, sent her husband out of the room on a wild goose chase, slipped out of the room to kill Phyllis, then came back to pretend she was asleep when her husband got back?"

Miles looked stunned. "Wow, you're good. I was thinking more along the lines of Mr. Franco went out to get the ice, ran into Phyllis, killed her, then got ice from the kitchen and went back to his sleeping wife."

"He's good, right?" Loralin asked Miles. "He's got a sharp analytical mind."

"He sure does," Miles agreed. "But in this case, we can prove that Mrs. Franco does have an ankle injury and would have been incapable of killing Phyllis and throwing her out of a window."

"Damn," Loralin and Devin said at once.

"So, is Mr. Franco now officially a suspect?"

Loralin sounded almost disappointed. Now they might have too many suspects.

"Technically yes," Miles informed them. "However, he says he saw someone coming out of Phyllis's room when he was letting himself back into his room."

Devin put his fork down and pushed his plate away, and Loralin picked up her wine glass and took a long swig. "Please tell me we know who the person is," she almost begged.

Miles barked a laugh. "For once, we might just be that lucky. The person seen coming out of Phyllis's room had on a hotel robe over a hoodie and jeans. He also had a phone which he spoke into. Mr. Franco heard him say, "It's done.""

"Well, I'll be damned," Loralin said, smacking the table. "We've got a murder for hire on our hands. And wasn't that what our last killer wore too? How unoriginal"

"Now that's something I never expected," Devin agreed. "So, does that mean Zoey and Hank are off the hook?"

"No," Miles said with a sigh. "We showed Mr. Franco a picture of Hank and he positively ID'd him as the person he saw leaving Phyllis's room."

Loralin and Devin were still contemplating the news they'd just gotten when Loralin's phone buzzed. "Hello, this is Loralin speaking."

"Hey, boss, this is Gage. Um… the police are here with a warrant to search Jeremy Orville's locker and any of the rooms he had access to. They also want to talk to people who knew Jeremy."

"Oh, okay, Gage. Since they have a warrant, just let them do what they have to do. And don't forget to tell them about the super close relationship Jeremy developed with Deke Robertson. I believe he's still staying with us." Both Devin and Miles noticed the evil grin on her face.

"Yes, ma'am. Thank you." Gage hung up the phone before he heard his boss's brief but powerful cackle of laughter.

"What did you do, Loralin?" Devin demanded before she'd

even set her phone back on the table.

"Nothing," she said innocently. "I just reported Jeremy missing and told them that he'd taken some stuff from the hotel that wasn't his."

Miles groaned. "Please tell me you didn't lie to get that warrant."

"I didn't get the warrant. Elk River PD did. But no, I didn't lie about Jeremy taking stuff from the inn. He has the uniform that is supposed to be returned, and there is a ring that went missing the other day."

"Loralin," Devin said, his voice coming out like a warning. "That ring was returned to the owner when it was found in a heating vent."

"Was it?" she asked innocently. "Wow, I never heard that."

"You two are going to get me fired," Miles fussed. "First, you get recognized while questioning suspects, and then you falsify information on a warrant."

Loralin scoffed. "I did not falsify anything. I thought the ring was still missing!"

Miles just rolled his eyes at his ex-wife. "Anyway, maybe by tomorrow we will have an end to this murder and to your vendetta against Deke Robertson."

Loralin stood and went after Miles, who had stood to clear the table. Devin held her back. "It's not a vendetta. He's planning something to hurt my inn, and I want to know what it is. His room being searched could scare him a little and make him sloppy."

"Okay, okay," Miles said, holding up his hands. "Just make sure you keep my name out of it and don't get Henderson in trouble. She might be my new partner after she takes the detective exam."

* * *

Everyone was in for a shock when Loralin and Devin arrived at work the next morning. She had a message on the work phone from Henderson. It seemed that there was no such person as Jeremy Orville. His social security number was fake, and no one had lived at the address he'd listed in the last year.

"So who was he?" Devin asked as he paced the floor inside Loralin's office. "And how did we not know?"

Loralin was fuming. "He obviously didn't want us to know who he was and had the resources to create an identity to fool us with. And I was so nice to that kid after Chef freaked out on him."

"We were all nice to him." Devin reminded her. "But why would he have to use a fake identity?"

"Because Deke didn't want us to be able to link them. I bet you a million bucks that if we could look into Deke's life in depth, we'd find Jeremy in there somewhere."

Devin found himself getting angrier by the minute. He hated being fooled, and he felt bad about thinking Loralin had overreacted to the whole Deke Robertson thing. "I'd like to give that kid a piece of my mind right about now."

"Yeah, well, let's hope Elk River PD can find him because I need to know what Deke has planned."

Devin stopped pacing and sat down. "Should we kick him out?"

Loralin stood and started pacing the room in Devin's place. "I'm not so sure. I mean, part of me wants to boot him out on his ass so he has no access to us. But the other part of me is insisting that we keep our enemy close."

***

Devin walked into Loralin's office just before lunchtime. He was feeling restless, angry, and sad. "Hey, can I ask you something?"

Loralin looked up from her computer and took off her glasses to look at him. "Of course. You know that."

"This is something a bit different." Devin sat down across from her and rubbed his hands along his thighs. "I… Can you… Will you go out with me tonight? I think maybe it will help if we have an official date. I mean, if you want. Maybe it won't help. I'm just going to keep finding excuses. Or maybe not. Just forget it. I mean, unless you want to."

Loralin smiled and reached across the desk to offer her hand. He took it. "You're babbling again. I would love to go out with you."

"Really?" he said shyly, unable to look her fully in the eyes.

"Yeah," she said. "I think it might be a good way to decide what we want, and the case is out of our hands for the moment."

"Good," he said, finally looking at her. "Any place you would prefer to go?"

"Actually," she said with a grin. "There is that new place in Cheyenne that I'm dying to try. It opens at four, and if we left soon, I could show you around Cheyenne, then we could get in early and be home before it's too late."

He had no idea what restaurant she was talking about, but a trip to finally see Cheyenne sounded fun, and it was only a couple of hours away. "Okay, sounds good. What should I wear?"

"Slacks and a button-up," she answered as she picked up the phone. "I'll make reservations."

Devin headed to the cottage to change, knowing Loralin wouldn't be too far behind. He felt so nervous for some reason, almost like it was his first date ever. It was because their friendship was what was clouding his feelings about her. He couldn't face the idea that any change in their status could ruin their original bond of friendship. This was something he couldn't mess up. This date had to go perfectly, or he felt he might never be able to look Loralin in the eyes again.

"You ready?" Loralin asked, lounging in the doorway of Devin's bedroom.

When he looked up, he nearly lost his breath. "Wow, you are so beautiful."

Loralin looked down, afraid to meet his gaze and see if he was telling the truth. "Thanks. You look pretty damn good yourself."

Devin felt his face flush. He was acting like a kid again, like when Ellie Pearson had leaned over and kissed him in their year 9 math class. "Want me to drive?" he asked. It was the safest question he could think of.

"Please." Loralin looped her arm through his, and they made their way to the back carport where his car awaited them. "Are you feeling unusually nervous, like this is a live-or-die situation?"

Devin laughed as some of the tension was eased. Holding the door open for Loralin, he kissed her cheek. "Yes. I thought for sure I was the only one feeling this way." He hurried around to the driver's side and climbed in. This would either be the best date ever or the one that ended his life with Loralin forever.

* * *

This was the first time Devin had ever driven to Cheyenne, and he suddenly knew what Loralin complained about all the time. It was the most boring drive of his life. It was a good thing he wasn't the least bit sleepy. "Man, this feels long."

"I know," Loralin sympathized. "I think of all the road trips I've taken in Wyoming, and there have been many, this is the worst one. But the company is fabulous, and from what I hear about the food at this new place, it's well worth the drive."

"So, this new place, I can't recall ever hearing about it." He had wracked his brain since she'd mentioned it and couldn't come up with a TV or paper ad to answer his questions.

"It's called Infinite. It's modern outside, but it has more of a down-home menu." Loralin told him. "Upscale down-home, apparently. I can't wait to see how they pull it off."

"What, like filet mignon and mashed taters with imported beer or something?" Devin was trying to define upscale down home.

"Maybe," she said with a shrug. "I guess we'll see. I mean, does that sound bad?"

Devin tried not to laugh. "It doesn't sound bad. A Prime cut of steak with the best kind of potatoes on the planet and an expensive, tasty beer. We could do worse."

Now it was Loralin's turn to keep from laughing. Sometimes she loved his way of seeing the world. He was still so young and, in some ways, so unencumbered by the ills of the world. "Is there anything in particular that you want to see first in Cheyenne?"

"How about the state museum?" he said without hesitation. "I find myself becoming more and more fascinated with the whole 'old time western' history theme, and I hear they have some great exhibits."

"They do. I swear we used to go there every year in school, and I never got tired of it." She was proud of her home state and had always wanted to show him everything she possibly could. They just hadn't had much time yet. He'd gotten there only a day before the grand opening, and with two murders and the Deke Robertson situation, there had been no time for fun. She was most likely going to see more of Tasmania when they went for a month than he would see of Wyoming after being there six months.

They were both quiet for a long time. Loralin figured they were only a few minutes away from town before Devin finally broke the comfortable silence. "So, do you want me to stop by police headquarters so you can talk to Don? You have a date coming up soon, right?"

Loralin had to look at him to see what kind of mood he was in. She saw a playful glint in his eyes. "Yes! Let's go see him. Maybe he can join us!"

She felt a change in the air coming from the driver's seat, so she risked a peek at Devin. His face was getting a bit red, and his breathing had increased. "Are you serious?" he ground out.

Loralin couldn't hold the laughter in anymore. "No, I'm not serious. Jealous much?"

Devin pouted and looked straight ahead at the road. "Not jealous."

Loralin knew that it wasn't worth arguing about it because he would never admit it until he admitted that he had feelings for her. "Okay, at the next street turn right, and it should be about a quarter of a mile down on the left."

Devin followed her instructions and pulled into a parking space. He knew he was being a nerd, but he was excited to see the museum. And Loralin seemed to feel the same. They started with the Wyoming Wildscapes exhibit and made their way through three other exhibits before they decided to save the rest for another day, so they could get to dinner.

"I had no idea the museum was so extensive," he said as they got back into the car. "Although, I guess I should have. A state would include the whole state's history."

"Yeah," Loralin agreed. "I didn't even think that we wouldn't be able to make it through the whole thing before closing and needing to make our reservation. One of these days, we will make a day of it and hit a lot of the sites in town."

"I'd like that," he said. "But you know, it would be nice to bring my dad and Trevor too."

"We will," she said, giving him a sweet smile. "Drive two blocks, then turn right, and it will be on the right."

Devin nodded and drove in silence. He knew he loved it there, and he knew that he didn't ever want to leave Loralin or Wyoming. So, why was it so hard to let himself feel what he wanted to feel for her? Was his mother's view on their relationship that important to him? It had never been before. In fact, he'd already chosen Loralin over his mother when he decided to take the manager's job and move to America. Every time she called from the women's prison in Lusk, though, he felt like an errant little child, and he wanted to make it up to his mother. That's why this date was so important. He was hoping it would set him on the right track and help him deal with his mother's guilt. "Wow, would you look at that," he said as they pulled into a parking space next to the restaurant. "It looks like one of those glass block houses you see on those real estate shows."

"I know," Loralin said. "I thought you might like that about it. I know your style runs more modern than mine."

"I can't wait to see inside,' he said as he walked around and opened her door for her. "I wonder if it's modern or down home."

"Maybe a mixture of both?" she hazarded a guess. You know down-home decor with modern high gloss finishes and appliances."

Devin's previous mood was gone, and he was walking into the restaurant with a genuine smile on his face. "Now that sounds interesting."

The entrance wasn't anything to write home about, but as soon as they stepped into the waiting area, the experience really began. It was as Loralin had imagined. The decor was simple and had a country flair. The calm but colorful walls invited you right in, and the floral and rustic decor made you want to stay, but the reservation desk and everything on it was the most modern model possible. "Hello, how can I help you?"

"We have a reservation for two at four o'clock," Devin said to the hostess who was dressed in a down-home, western uniform.

"And the name," she returned.

"Wentworth," Loralin piped in.

"Okay," the young woman said, grabbing two menus from a nearby glass and chrome stand. "Follow me."

Devin was quite impressed. The furnishings were all made of old and distressed wood, but the dishes and stemware were all modern, appeared to be real silver, and were shining. Once they were seated, he picked up the menu and looked it over. "Loralin, do you want filet mignon and mashed taters with gravy and mixed vegetables? And then you can get the imported beer and make it come full circle."

"Are you serious?" she asked, finally picking up the menu.

"Dead serious," he said with a chuckle. "I think that's exactly what I'm going to have."

Loralin put the menu down. "Let's make that two."

When the waiter came around to take their drink orders, Devin ordered two of their most expensive imported beers and then two of the filet mignon dinners. It was easy to tell that the waiter was new to waiting tables, and he looked grateful for the simple but quick order.

"Maybe we should have waited to come here," Loralin said. "I'm so hungry, and new restaurants can have longer wait times because they are just so busy."

"Well, I don't think we have to worry about that," Devin said, putting his napkin in his lap. "Our food only took fifteen minutes and twenty-four seconds."

"What?" she said, looking behind her. Their waiter was headed toward their table with their food on his shiny chrome serving tray. "You actually timed it?"

Devin laughed. "Yeah, I was hungry and had the same thought as you, so I timed it."

Loralin loved these little quirks that Devin had. He'd once timed how long it took to be seated in a restaurant after the host had said fifteen to twenty minutes. When he heard Loralin say that she was hurting and wanted to just sit and eat, he timed them. But he wasn't the one who complained when 45 minutes went by before they were seated. That was something she always did, so he left her to it. "So, they seated us quickly, brought us our food quickly, and served one of the best beers I've ever tasted. So far so good."

Devin reached over and took her hand. "I'm wondering if anything can mess up this date." He then leaned in and kissed her straight on the lips. That was something he'd never done outside of their home.

"Loralin Robbins! Fancy seeing you here." Both of them recognized the voice.

"Don Peterson, what are you doing here?" Loralin wondered if he had seen her kissing Devin.

"I came here to try it out. All of my poker buddies were curious." He pointed to the men two tables away. "I couldn't believe my eyes when I saw you here."

"Oh yeah, well, Devin and I are trying to date a bit and decided to make an afternoon of it here in Cheyenne." Loralin felt bad because she was supposed to go out with Don soon, and at that very moment, she had no desire to do it. She preferred Devin's company in every way.

"Oh, uh, I see," he said, a frown on his brow. "I'd hate to interfere with your date."

"I uh," Loralin wasn't sure what she should say. She didn't want to scare Devin off by declaring them a couple, but she didn't exactly want to go through with the date with Don either.

"She'll let you know if she's with me exclusively by the time your date rolls around," Devin said with a stony voice.

"Well then, I guess that's fair," Don said with a strained smile. "Enjoy your dinner."

"Thank you, Don," Loralin said. "I'll talk to you soon."

Devin blew out the breath he'd been holding. "Was that too rude?" he asked.

"No," Loralin told him. "It was a bit serious, and your tone could have been a smidge gentler, but no, it wasn't rude."

"Good," he said. "You can call him tomorrow and let him know that you won't be able to go on the date with him."

"Excuse me?" Loralin barked in a whisper. "Are you telling

me that we will be exclusive by tomorrow, or are you just being a jealous buffoon and telling me I can't go out with Don if you haven't made up your mind yet?"

Devin had the good grace to look embarrassed. "Well, I, fine, you can go out with him if we aren't exclusive. But I'm going to be there at another table, so he can't grope you."

Loralin wasn't sure if she should smile or laugh, or punch him in the nose. "You know, jealousy doesn't look good on you."

"It's not jealousy," he said softly, through gritted teeth. "It's one person's concern for the other."

"Bull shit," she snapped back. "I already know what you want from our relationship, but you're too damn stubborn to see it."

"I don't want anything from it," he said, standing and motioning for the waiter. "Check, please."

Loralin sat there with her mouth agape until the waiter showed up with their check. Then she stood and followed Devin out of the restaurant. "What the hell is your problem?"

He turned on her and clasped her upper arms. "My problem is that I love you, but I know I shouldn't. I don't know what to do, Loralin, and if you can't be patient, then maybe there is nothing more to talk about."

She was stunned as she walked to the car and opened her door. "All I did was tell you that you're jealous of Don, and you freak out and accuse me of not being patient? Am I not allowed to talk about it? Am I not allowed to try to help you realize what you are thinking so we can get this over and done with?"

Devin sat there in the driver's seat and let his head fall to the steering wheel. "God Loralin, I'm sorry. This is just so important to me. But I spent the last so many years being told by the strongest woman in my life that what I felt was wrong. That a simple friendship with a woman twenty years older than me was wrong. How am I supposed to sort through that when every time I see you all I want to do is hold you, spend every moment with you, make love to you every day for the rest of my life."

"I think that's your answer, Devin."

He guffawed. "You'd think so, huh? But it's not that simple. I can't bring myself to make that one last decision, to give us that one last label because my mother, of all people, told me not to."

They were both quiet for some time when Devin started up the car and pulled out of the lot. "I..."

"Don't," Loralin said softly. "You don't have to speak. I'll be patient while you work through this, but remember, I'm an old lady and I won't be alive and sexy for much longer."

This made Devin burst into laughter, and the tension in the car was broken. "So, when you get home, do you want to stop at The Scooperia and get a gallon of our favorite mint-chip ice cream and go home and drown our sorrows?"

"Sounds like a plan to me," she answered. She could probably eat a whole gallon herself. She might splurge for two gallons.

* * *

The ice cream didn't get eaten that night, though. It was carelessly tossed in the big freezer on the carport when Loralin received a phone call that she hoped to never get again.

"Hey, Loralin, it's Maureen. There's been another murder. A guest found Jeremy's body about a quarter of a mile into the woods behind the inn. He'd been shot and tossed into some undergrowth."

"Fuck!" Loralin rarely ever dropped the f-bomb, but she figured this was one occasion that called for it.

"What's wrong?" Devin asked as he unpacked their bag of ice cream.

Loralin told him what Maureen had said, and they both grabbed a tub of ice cream and walked it out to the freezer before working their way around the house to the path that led to the inn.

For once, Devin couldn't read her. "What's on your mind?"

"Maybe selling this place to Deke isn't such a bad idea. It may be cursed, and I would be happy to curse that man." She was walking slowly as if she didn't want to have to deal with this situation anytime soon.

"I feel ya, but it's not cursed. It's just how things are, right now. I'm sure once this murder is solved, that will be the last one for a while." He could only hope.

"Only because I won't be here," Loralin said with a sigh. "I'll be in Tasmania cursing your family's hotel and turning it into the murder hotel of Australia."

Devin knew better than to argue when she was in this mood. Nothing would convince her that she wasn't cursed until she decided that she wasn't. Hopefully, that will be soon.

When they arrived at the inn, Miles was inside talking to people, and Loralin walked straight up to him. "So…"

"So," Miles returned. "I have no idea. We don't know if this is random, if it is related to Phyllis, or what. All we know is that we had a missing person, and he was found dead. At least we can get a positive ID when we get the results of his fingerprints back."

"Well, that's good news," Devin said, looking over at Loralin.

He hated seeing her so beaten down. If there wasn't a break in one of the cases soon, she might just explode.

"Can you question Devin and me next?" she said with a yawn. "We had a long day in Cheyenne, and I want to go home and go to bed."

"I bet," Miles said with a chuckle.

"I meant to sleep, you big jerk." Loralin was not in a joking mood.

"Touchy touchy. Come on into your office, and I'll question you so you can 'sleep'."

Loralin followed him, and Devin stayed by her side so there wouldn't be yet another murder at The Robbins' Nest Inn.

14

Surveillance Expert Loralin Robbins

Loralin and Devin headed home after they were questioned. The police and the state forensics team were concentrating their efforts outside where the body was found, so she didn't feel the need to stick around. Miles would keep her up to date on the investigation. For some reason, Loralin didn't feel the usual rush she got after there was a case to solve. At this point, she didn't want anything to do with the second murder.

It wasn't until the next morning, over breakfast, that she realized she had a stake in the second murder too. Deke and Jeremy had been up to something at her inn, and now one of them was dead. "What's so special about my inn that someone would have died?" she murmured to Devin as she poured them both a second cup of coffee.

"Do you want to rephrase that?" he asked with a hint of amusement. "It seems that your inn is the happening place to be murdered."

Loralin felt herself blush a little. "Okay, what I meant was what is so special about my inn that someone would get murdered while trying to help Deke Robertson increase his property count?"

"Better," Devin laughed. "And truthfully, I don't know. We still have no idea what they have been up to. I mean, I halfway expected a kitchen full of roaches or mice or an exploding sewer system by now, but nothing has gone wrong."

"I know," Loralin murmured. But today she was going to find out. "I think I'm going to come into the office and grab a few things and then take the rest of the morning off. I should be back by the afternoon."

"Okay," Devin said as he put his dishes in the sink and grabbed his wallet off the counter. "I'm going to be doing interviews for people to replace Zoey, Hank, and Jeremy."

"Being a housekeeper here is bad news," Loralin mused. "Penny was murdered, Jeremy was murdered, and Zoey and Hank are being held for murder."

Devin prayed she hadn't just jinxed him. There had to be people out there who wouldn't put two and two together and still want to work housekeeping, right? At least he hoped the hell so, or he'd be doing double duty, cleaning rooms and running the rest of the inn. "I was going to say wish me luck, but I need more than just a wish."

* * *

Loralin went into her office, grabbed her binoculars, and the notebook with the complaints about Deke and Jeremy. She was going to follow the hotelier and see if she could find out something. Where exactly did he go all day, and why didn't he just commute from Casper now that the detours were gone? The first thing she needed to do was see if Heather would lend her her car. She dialed her daughter's phone, but no one answered. Next, she tried her ex-husband.

"This is Miles." He sounded grumpy. She decided not to let on where she was going or what she was doing. He'd just get grumpier and forbid her to go.

"Hey, have you seen Heather? I need to borrow something from her." There, that was something safe to say.

"Yeah, she should be arriving at the inn soon. She left here about ten minutes ago. We got an ID back on Jeremy Orville."

"Oh, well, that's nice." Ooh, she sounded too fake there. "That's great. Who was he really?"

"His real name is Elijah Montrose. He's originally from Denver and worked as a housekeeper at one of Deke Robertson's upscale properties in Casper."

That didn't make sense to Loralin. "What was an upscale housekeeper doing working in a small-town inn? And was that the only connection he had to Deke?"

"I don't know," Miles told her. "We haven't found any other connection yet."

"Okay," Loralin said with a sigh. "I've got to go. I'll talk to you later. Keep me updated."

"Will do." Miles hung up.

Loralin left her office and went in search of her daughter. She guessed she'd either be in the dining room or hanging around the front desk. "Hey, kiddo."

"Hey, Mama. What's up?" The young woman hugged her mother.

"I was wondering if I could borrow your car." She hoped she wouldn't have to explain why or make up an excuse about why she couldn't use her own car.

"Sure! Can Hanna and I borrow your car? We're going

to Casper to do some shopping and want to have plenty of room in the back for our purchases." Loralin loved seeing her daughter so animated and unstressed.

"Sounds good. You can pick up your car this evening when you get back from town." They hugged each other and then exchanged keys. Before anyone could stop her or say anything that might delay her, Loralin raced out of the inn and jumped in Heather's car.

She wasn't technically going anywhere yet, but she didn't want to be inside the inn when she started to follow Deke. He usually had breakfast in his room around eight o'clock, and by half past, he was heading to his car. This day was no exception.

"Where are you going and what are you up to?" she whispered when he finally got in his car and pulled out of the lot. Loralin took it slow and made sure to stay back several car lengths. She'd never done much trailing or surveillance, but how hard could it be? She'd read so many mystery books that she could probably do it in her sleep.

It didn't surprise her when Deke drove away from Elk River and headed toward Boone. It did, however, surprise her when he bypassed the county seat and headed toward the nearby town of Wheatland.

She was a little bit more nervous about following someone on the freeway, and if he was headed to Wheatland, they would be on I-25 for about an hour. "You can do this," she told herself out loud in the car. "Just don't get too close and don't lose him." And that's what she did.

There was enough traffic in the town that it was easy for her to keep her distance. Luckily, she had spent a few summer months with her friend Marcy in Wheatland when she was a child, so she knew the town pretty well. They didn't have any major hotel properties that Deke would be interested in, so she just couldn't figure out where he might be going. The biggest shock of the whole trip was when he pulled into the parking lot of the Southern Wyoming Care Center, a nursing home. Why had he been visiting a nursing home for weeks, and why had he chosen her inn to stay at while he did it? And how was Jeremy involved? This seemed like a much bigger mystery than the death of Phyllis Palmer.

Tying a scarf around her head and putting sunglasses on, she shot out of the car and headed through the door where Deke had just disappeared. While he was at the desk, she tried to catch what he was saying to the woman, but they were talking too quietly. Once he had been buzzed back into the resident's area, Loralin moved out of the shadows and approached the desk. The woman who had been there must have been escorting Deke to the person he was visiting.

Looking around to make sure that no one could see her and that there were no cameras in the waiting room, she reached under the plexiglass shield and pulled the sign-in log closer. The name next to Deke's signature, Veronica Patchelli, meant nothing to her.

The hair stood up on Loralin's neck, telling her someone was coming, so she pulled away from the plexiglass, but before she could turn and rush out, the woman was back at the desk. "Can I help you?"

"Uh, yeah, I hope so. My jerk of a brother put our father in a care center, and he didn't tell me which one. Do you have a patient by the name of Harold Perkins?" She prayed that there was no one living there by that name.

"No, I'm sorry, we don't. Have you tried the care centers in Glendo or Gurnsey?"

"I haven't yet," Loralin said with a big smile. "I guess I'll try there tomorrow. Thank you." She turned and walked out the door and went straight to Heather's Car. She wondered how long she'd have to wait until Deke came out. Maybe he was just visiting here and went somewhere work-related after lunch.

It was noon on the dot when Deke exited the care center and got in his car. She waited a few minutes and then followed him. He ended up at the local diner, where he met with a man whom Loralin didn't recognize.

Watching them get and eat their food was killing her. She was starving but didn't dare go into the small building. He'd see her for sure. Looking around, she noticed a convenience store across the street. It wasn't ideal, but a gas station sandwich and a bottled drink would have to do for her lunch.

She was done eating and trying hard not to doze off when Deke and the man left the restaurant. As an afterthought, she pulled out her camera and took a picture of the two men as they got into Deke's car. Maybe Miles or someone else in Elk River would recognize him.

This time, when he left the diner, he didn't head back to the Care Center, and Loralin started to get excited. This was it. She could finally find out what he was up to. But when he again stopped the car, it wasn't where she had expected. He pulled up in front of a tiny house on the outskirts of town and went inside with the man from the diner. Now she was even more curious, but also more puzzled. What the hell was Deke up to, and how did it have anything to do with The Robbin's Nest Inn?

Loralin waited in her car for a few minutes, then decided to get out. There were windows shadowed by trees on the west side of the house. She could sneak in there and maybe see what was going on inside.

Two steps into the grass, and a twig snapped. She stood motionless, holding her breath until her fear subsided, and then she continued on. Once she was snuggled safely in the trees, she took out the binoculars she'd brought with her and looked in the window. Deke and the man from the diner were arguing. She could hear them saying something about the boy being sloppy and not worth the money. But what job was he talking about? Securing her inn for himself? Something was going on, and it didn't appear to be what she thought it was. At that moment, she wished she'd had Devin come with her. Maybe they could have bounced ideas off each other.

Loralin decided she'd seen and heard enough; she wasn't going to learn anything by following Deke anymore. As she moved slowly out of the trees, she heard a dog bark and started to walk faster. "There's a woman in them bushes!" she heard the man from the diner holler. She wasn't sure whether to keep moving fast or to make an all-out run for her car across the street. Her body decided for her as she found herself running and hoping her disguise didn't fail her. They would know someone had been spying, but not who it was.

Just before she reached the door of Heather's car, she heard a loud crack and felt burning in her left arm. The driver-side back window shattered. "Damn it, stop shooting, you fool!" Deke's voice sounded like it was spoken in slow motion.

Loralin didn't stop to find out what exactly was going on; she just jumped in the car and took off. It wasn't until she had left Wheatland's city limits that she realized she had been shot in the arm. There was blood everywhere, and she suddenly felt dizzy. "Alexa, call 911." The last thing she remembered was putting on the brakes and her head hitting the steering wheel.

15

Gunshot Wounds, Love, & Other Things

"Ma'am, can you hear me?" Someone was talking to Loralin, but who? She didn't see anyone. In fact, she couldn't see anyone or anything, so she opened her eyes. "What happened?"

"You were shot," said the kind female voice she'd heard just a moment before. "And you bonked your head. I think we should transport you to Cheyenne." The paramedic was looking in her eyes with one of those little lights, and it hurt.

"No, I, I'm okay." She looked down at the bandage on her arm and then back up at the paramedic. "It doesn't look like the gunshot is a big deal, and I feel fine. I'll just head home to Elk River."

"Ma'am, I can't let you do that," the other paramedic said. "You lost consciousness, and I think you probably have a concussion. Please let us transport you to Cheyenne so we don't have to come rescue you from a traffic accident a few miles down the road."

A sudden wave of dizziness hit her, and Loralin allowed the

female paramedic to lay her back on the gurney. "Fine, fine. Is there any way you could transport me to Campbell County instead? I don't want my family to have to come all the way to Cheyenne to pick me up."

The male paramedic, who seemed to be the one in charge, walked away and got on his radio. After a few minutes, he came back. "Campbell doesn't have any available ambulances to send out this way, ma'am."

"Call the Chief of Police in Cheyenne and tell him that Loralin needs a ride to the hospital." She had her eyes closed and didn't plan on changing that for a while. She was too dizzy.

"What?" the paramedic said, looking at his partner. "Why would I do that?"

"Just do it!" Loralin demanded sitting up and then instantly regretted it.

Within a half hour, Don Peterson himself showed up and had the paramedics escort her to the cruiser he'd come in. "I hate to sound like your ex-husband," Don said. "But what on earth were you doing that got you shot? You need to be more careful."

"Don't even start with me, Don. I was just trying to find out what Deke Robertson was up to, and I ran into trouble." She didn't feel up to talking to him about this. Especially when her ex-husband's rival was sounding exactly like her ex-husband.

"Deke did this?" Don Snarled. "I'll have him arrested!"

Loralin sighed and rested her weary head against the window of the cruiser. "Deke didn't do this. And please don't. I need to know what in the hell he's up to."

"It's not worth risking your life for, Loralin," Don demanded. "What, did he try to steal the inn or something?"

Do you know Deke?" Loralin said softly, to not hurt her

head.

"Everyone in the state knows that snake," Don said. "He'd sell his own mother for gas money. The only person in this world I think he truly loved was Veronica Montrose Patchelli. At least until she left town on him almost thirty years ago, now I believe."

"Wait. Explain yourself. Who was this Veronica Patchelli?"

"His first wife. They got married and were set to live happily ever after, running his first hotel, The Country Inn in Casper. But then she got sick and disappeared, and he's never been the same."

One by one, things began to fall into place in her mind, but a few things were missing, and she wasn't sure how to get the information she needed. "Thanks for bringing me here," Loralin said as they pulled into the emergency department of Campbell County's hospital. "I just really didn't want to be stuck in Cheyenne when Boone is a half hour from home."

"I understand," Don said with a smile. "Now let's get you inside and settled in, and you can call that family of yours so they don't get worried."

Don Peterson might have been a handsy SOB, but when it came down to it, he could be a sweet and caring man. The last time she'd been hospitalized, during the first murder at the inn, he'd gone to the ends of the earth to find her and even arranged to have her car towed home. Speaking of which. "Don, what happened to my daughter's car?"

"It's being gone over by the police in Wheatland, and then it will be turned over to the Elk River PD." He patted her hand, then got out of the car and walked into the hospital, only to appear a few moments later with a nurse and a wheelchair. "Alright, Loralin. I'm going to entrust these kind people with you and head back to Cheyenne to do some work."

Loralin sighed as she transferred over to the wheelchair. "You're going after Deke, aren't you?"

"I'm sure he's long gone back home by now," Don said, "but if you would be so kind as to tell me exactly who shot you and where I might find him, I am going to go arrest that son of a bitch."

Loralin thought long and hard, wondering if she could be honest with Don without messing up her investigation into Deke. "It was a man that Deke met at Mary's diner in Wheatland. They then went to a house at 4312 Balm Street."

"Skeeter Jones?" Don asked, then shook his head. "That man is bound and determined to get himself a jail sentence. He's Wheatland's town drunk and troublemaker. I think I'll go pay him a visit. He probably won't remember anything, but they did find the bullet casing in your daughter's car."

"Thanks again, Don," Loralin said as she started to be wheeled away. "And be careful!"

* * *

Loralin was cleaned up, had a bandage on the wound where the bullet grazed her, and was sitting up in the hospital bed they had assigned to her. It was time to call Devin and hope like hell he would agree to come get her.

"Loralin, where are you?" He was already worried. He'd probably insist she stay in the hospital for a week.

"Now don't freak out, but I'm at the Campbell County Medical Complex, and I need you to grab all of my files on Deke. I already have the notebook we started, but I'll need the research the attorney gave me. Oh, and grab the files on

Phyllis's murder and bring them to me."

"Are you out of your mind?!" he screeched into the phone. "You're in the hospital? What happened? And where have you been all day?"

"I'm fine, Devin. I was grazed by a bullet and hit my head on the steering wheel. I was following Deke, and things went a little sideways. Can you please gather my stuff and come get me?"

"Oh, I'll gather your stuff and be right there, but I know you, and unless the doctor says you can leave, I'm not letting you out of that room." He hung up the phone.

Loralin sure hoped he'd remember to call Miles and her daughters. She still didn't know how to tell Heather about her back window. And sure enough, just over half an hour later, she heard a siren come to a stop outside and moved from the bed to look. Miles, Devin, and Hanna all filed out of his police cruiser. Heather, no doubt, wouldn't be far behind.

* * *

Loralin braced herself when the door opened, and everyone filed in. They would either all chew her out at once or make sure she was okay, then chew her out. She would bet on the first option, though, because she didn't exactly look like she was in bad shape.

The door opened, and she held up her hand. "I don't want to hear it. I know I shouldn't have gone off on my own, and I know I should have been more careful. But it's over now, and I'm okay. So if you want to come in to visit, then welcome. If not, you can turn around and leave."

Devin noticed that Miles was about to turn around and leave, but when he looked at his daughter, he decided against it. "How are you feeling?" Devin wanted to know.

"I'm okay. I've got a sore arm and a hell of a headache." She didn't mention that her mind was racing and she couldn't wait for them to leave so she could go through her files and possibly solve both cases she'd been working on.

"You had us worried sick," he said as he bent down and kissed her cheek. "The thought that I could have lost you…"

Loralin reached up and caressed his cheek. "I'm here, and I'm fine. We'll talk later, okay?" Devin nodded and let Heather and Miles stand next to her bedside.

"Hey, Mama. I'm so glad you're okay. When can you come home?" She hated seeing her child so worried. What she'd done wasn't that big of a deal, was it? She'd done similar stuff for her whole married life when she'd helped Miles with his cases. But she'd never actually been shot.

"They want to keep me overnight for observation because of a concussion. I'm one hundred percent okay, though. I think I'll leave after I get some strength back."

"No, you won't," Miles grumbled. "Devin is under strict orders from the Elk River PD that you are to stay here until a doctor releases you tomorrow."

Loralin wanted to tell Miles that he was ridiculous if he thought that could keep her here. But she kept her mouth closed. She didn't want to cause trouble; she just wanted her life back and to travel to Tasmania with the man she loved. And she did love him. Somewhere along the way, she'd fallen in love with the one person she wasn't supposed to. Everybody kept telling her and warning her that it had happened, and she kept denying it. But there was something about a gunshot ringing in your ears that cleared your mind. "Well, I'm going to talk to the doctor and see if he'll change his mind because I need to get out of here. I think I'm on the verge of solving a murder or two and the mystery of Deke Robertson staying at my hotel for so long."

"And that can wait until you get home tomorrow, Loralin," Miles insisted. "You need to take care of yourself for your family, and that includes Devin."

"Maybe," she said just to shut him up.

"Are we having a party?" the doctor asked as he came into the room and smiled at the occupants. "Could you give me a few minutes alone with my patient, and then you can continue to party the night away?"

Loralin loved the doctor. He had such a flirty personality and a great sense of humor. Maybe she could use her flirtiness to get him to bend to her will. "So, doctor," she said with her cutest smile. "Is there any way I can get you to let me out of here tonight?" Her expression was between begging and pouting. "Please."

The doctor looked into her eyes and listened to her heart. "I really can't recommend you going home tonight, Mrs. Robbins. You have a pretty nasty bump on your head, and we need to keep an eye on it for a while."

"Come on, I promise not to do too much. I'll just lie in bed, and my friend and I will look over some paperwork until bedtime. Please."

"The only way you will be going home tonight is against medical advice. I'm sorry." He paused. "But, there is something I can do for you? I can permit your friend to stay here with you for the night as long as you promise not to get out of that bed."

"Fine," Loralin finally agreed. "I guess that will have to do."

She wasn't happy, and she might still leave against medical advice, but for now, she would stay and humor her family and the doctors.

When everyone came back in, Miles and Hanna brought Heather with them. "Oh, Mama, I'm so glad you're okay," Heather said, hugging her.

"I'm fine, sweetheart, but your car, not so much."

"I know," Heather said with a smile. "Don Peterson called me. I'll just need a new passenger window. I'd rather have to replace that than have you hurt or dead."

The two women hugged again, and Miles and Hanna took a turn. "We're going to head out," he said. "We're going to grab some dinner in town and head home. Devin will be back in the morning to bring you home."

"Actually, the doctor said that Devin can stay with me tonight. It's the only way he kept me from leaving."

Miles rolled his eyes and then laughed. "Okay then. We will see you tomorrow. Devin, make sure you take care of her, and don't let her move from that bed!"

"Yes, sir," Devin saluted. "Drive safe."

Once everyone was gone, Devin pulled up a chair and sat next to Loralin's hospital bed. He seemed at a loss for words until they just started to pour out. "You scared me to death. I tried calling you, and you didn't answer, and I had no idea where you'd gone."

"I know," Loralin said, caressing his cheek. "I'm sorry. I should have told someone where I'd be, but I just didn't know exactly where the day would take me."

"I would have come with you to follow Deke!" he insisted. "I could have helped."

Loralin sat with her hand in her lap, just staring at them. "Or

I could have gotten you killed or injured, too."

Devin reached over and turned her chin so she was looking at him. "You know, there is nothing like hearing the words 'I've been grazed by a bullet' to make one's mind clear on what is going on in their complicated world."

"I know," she whispered. "My complicated world suddenly became clear, too."

"I love you, Loralin. And I don't mean like just your best friend. I mean, I'm in love with you. I don't know how or exactly when it happened, but this whole time, everyone was right. My mother, my friends, everyone!"

"Good," she said somewhere between laughter and tears. "Because I'm in love with you too."

"Really?"

She loved it when he got excited about something, like a child on Christmas. "Yes. I don't know what the age difference means or how it even matters most of the time, but I'm willing to work through it with you. I… I mean, if you are."

"I am," he said with a smile. And although he'd never admit it, his eyes were misty too. "But there is something I need to ask you."

"Okay…" she didn't like the sound of that.

"Can we keep this just between us until we get back from Tasmania? Well, except for my mother. I have to go tell her before we leave."

"Sure, that's fine with me. Is there a specific reason you want to keep it quiet?"

"Yeah," he said, his face brightening. "This is going to be complicated enough without everyone in town saying 'I told you so' or 'I knew it!" I think it's just best if we get to know each other in this new way without that pressure. No one in

Tasmania will care, so we can solidify things in peace and then come back here and face the people who won't want to let us live it down."

"I like that idea," Loralin said with a yawn. "And what about your mother? Is there a reason you want to tell her before we leave?"

Devin yawned after she did, then sat up straighter in his chair. "I need to tell my mother that we are in love and let her know that she no longer has power over that decision. She no longer has a say in whether I admit my feelings or not."

Loralin was so glad to hear those last words. His mother had hated the thought of her and Devin possibly being together enough to want her dead, and she knew that you always weighed on his mind. "We'll go to Lusk to visit her before we leave for Tasmania."

"Knock knock," came a quiet voice from the doorway. "I'm from Uber Eats. I have two steak dinners with all the trimmings from The Porterhouse."

"For us?" Loralin asked. Who would have sent them steak dinners in the hospital?

"If your name is Loralin Robbins, yes."

"Oh, okay, thank you."

Devin took the bags of food from the young driver and tipped her before setting them out on the counter by the sink. Loralin signed for the delivery. "I can't imagine Miles spending this much money on us. Could it have been your girls?" he questioned.

"It was Don Peterson," Loralin said with a short laugh. "He sent a message to the driver. It says, 'Congratulations on finding someone as special as your young man. It's always better to be best friends before you become lovers. You're off the hook for our date, but maybe we can all get together and have lunch when I come for my interview. Word has it that we will be having reason to celebrate."

Devin laughed. "He always comes through. He really isn't a bad guy. We do need to find him a woman, though, so he can stop being known as Handsy Don."

"I couldn't agree more," Loralin stated. "But right now, I'm hungry as hell. Let's eat, and then we can get to work on solving these cases."

* * *

After dinner was cleaned up, Loralin and Devin were lucky they could move. "He sure went all out," she said. "That was a five-course meal."

"And it was so good," Devin said through a burp. "Excuse me!"

"So, where did you put the files?"

"Do we have to?" Devin moaned. "Can't we just vegetate until morning and then work on the case?"

"No!" Loralin acted offended that he would even suggest such a thing. "I want to get this done before I forget what I was thinking. Besides, I don't know how long Cheyenne and Elk River PDs can wait before they arrest the man who shot me, the man who was there when it happened."

"Alright, alright," he gave in as he stood up and moved to the counter by the sink and grabbed the folders and laptop he'd brought. "What exactly is it we are looking for?"

"Search for the surnames Montrose and Patchelli." She already had one of the file folders opened and was skimming it.

"For which thing?" he asked. "The murder or the snake in the grass." "Both," she murmured.

Devin wasn't sure he wanted to contemplate what that could mean. He didn't want to get too excited that it all could be over soon. "Okay, if you say so." He decided to start with the computer files, where for many of them he could do a search for just the name and wouldn't have to skim the whole file.

Loralin had looked through almost all of the paper files she had. There were only two left to go. "I must have been wrong," she said with a yawn. I swore I'd heard the name Montrose before in one of Phyllis's files."

"Do you even have all of her files? I know only parts of them were copied for us to use as paper copies. Let me do a search." Devin closed out of the Deke Robertson files he'd been checking through and opened the ones they'd written on Phyllis. "Here it is!"

Loralin sat up straighter in bed and leaned over toward Devin. "What does it say?"

"It says there were three closed files from nursing school. One was the Petterman file, the other was the Smith file, and the third one was the Montrose file."

Loralin fell back into the pillows that were propping her up. "Damn it. Those are files the warrant didn't give us access to."

"Okay, so wait a minute. I think I'm missing something. What does the name Montrose have to do with anything?"

Loralin had completely forgotten that she hadn't passed along what Miles had told her about Jeremy. "Jeremy Orville's real name was Elijah Montrose. And Deke's ex-wife's maiden name is Montrose."

"Wait, what?" Devin said, trying to remember if he'd ever heard about this ex-wife. What does Deke's ex-wife have to do with anything?"

"I followed Deke, and it appears he's been visiting his ex-wife, Veronica, in a nursing home this whole time. She is listed as Veronica Montrose Patchelli. And as for what she and Elijah have to do with each other, I have no clue, but I'm going to find out."

"Wow, that's strange," Devin said, not quite sure what to think.

"According to Don, everyone thought his wife had left him and disappeared. But it seems that she is living in Wheatland at the care center."

"Okay," Devin said. "So, we need to figure out what, if any, correlation Elijah and Veronica have to the Montrose in Phyllis's nursing school files."

"Yeah, and I'm not sure how I'm going to do that," Loralin said, looking off into space. "Can you keep checking for the name Patchelli? It rings a bell too, but I'm not sure from where."

Devin did as she asked, but a half hour later, the only file left was one filled with newspaper clippings about Deke that Jackson Fairway had given Loralin. "You want me to look through those, or do you want to do it?" he asked.

"I'll do it. Could you run down to the vending machine and get me some snacks and a Coke?"

Devin laughed. "I can't believe you're hungry again."

"Well, I am. Now go, please." Loralin was lost in thought when she heard the door close behind him.

When Devin came back to the room with an armful of snacks and drinks, Loralin was up and out of bed. She was pacing and had the biggest smile he'd ever seen on her face. "I know who killed Phyllis Palmer and Elijah Montrose, and damned if I don't know why Deke Robertson has been hanging around my inn!

Devin put the snacks on the tray on wheels that was over Loralin's bed. "Well, are you going to tell me?"

"Not yet," she said with one of her sassy grins. "We are going to get out of here, and you are going to drive me to Miles's house, and I will tell everyone at the same time. I don't feel like repeating myself."

"Loralin," Devin said through his gritted teeth. "Get back in bed. We will go see Miles in the morning, but there is no way I'm taking you anywhere tonight. I'm not going to lose you so soon after I found you."

"Damn it, Devin. Please." She was getting grumpy. "It's just a concussion."

"And concussions can kill. We are not leaving. Now, lie down and eat your snacks."

"Fine," she snarled. "But I'm not going to tell you who the murderer is until tomorrow, then."

He thought she was so cute when she pouted. "Okay," he said as if he wasn't bothered by her decision. "But save some of those snacks for me. I'm going to the bathroom, and then we are going to eat and go to bed." He heard her growl as he left the room.

16

It's A Family Affair

The minute Loralin woke up, she started to pace and fidget. She wouldn't listen to Devin and just rest until they left, and even the nurses told her she wouldn't be out of there until right after lunch.

"You're driving me crazy," he mumbled for the thirtieth time. "Could you please sit down and just wait until they release you?"

"I don't want to," she pouted.

"Don't make me force you. You are driving me and the nurses insane!"

"Fine," she grumbled and crawled back onto the bed. If the killer gets away, it will be your fault."

"The killer isn't going to get away unless you called them and accused them overnight. They don't know that you solved the case."

Loralin just ignored him and started a game on her phone. It would at least keep her busy until they brought her lunch. And as soon as they did, she shoved most of it in her mouth, took a long drink of milk, and marched out to the nurse's station, demanding to be released.

Devin gave up. He wasn't going to stop her. He was getting antsy, too, and he wanted to get back home with their friends and family. When he walked out of the room to see what she was doing, he found her signing the release papers, so he turned around and went back to the room to gather her stuff for her.

"Let's go," she said, turning to find him standing there. "Do not stop until we are at Elk River PD. I've already called Miles and told him to meet us there in half an hour."

"Yes, ma'am." He saluted. "Next stop Elk River PD."

* * *

It felt like Devin had barely parked when Loralin threw the door open and made a run for the entrance of police headquarters. Henderson was at the watch desk and saw her coming. "He said to tell you to go on in."

Loralin nodded and smiled at the woman, then veered slightly to the left. Devin had barely caught up with her when she stepped foot inside Miles's office. "So, are you ready to hear who killed Phyllis and Elijah?"

"Enlighten me," Miles said with a smile.

"Okay," Loralin started. "About twenty years ago, a man named Deacon Patchelli married a woman named Veronica Montrose. A short time later, she got sick and entered a teaching hospital in Montana."

"Okay," Miles said. He was not really impressed yet. "And?"

"And," Loralin said. "Shortly after the hospital stay, the wife disappeared. The man said she'd left him."

"Okay, keep going," Devin encouraged. "What does this have to do with Phyllis?"

"Well, that I'm not quite sure about," she said. "But I can guess. You see that man, Deacon Patchelli changed his name to Deke Robertson and used the money from a lawsuit with the hospital to open his second hotel in Casper, Wyoming."

"That's interesting," Miles said as he stood to pace. "And I'm assuming that you think Phyllis had something to do with his wife's health issues?"

"Yes," she stated. "Veronica Montrose Patchelli is alive but not so well in a nursing home in Wheatland. And Deke has been going there for weeks now. You see, Phyllis was a student nurse at that hospital, and the file about what happened to Deke's wife was sealed and not included in the warrant. I just need you to help us get access to it."

"It's not going to be easy," Miles said. "But go on."

"Well, I think if we can connect Deke to Phyllis, maybe we can find out if he hired Elijah to murder her."

"Elijah?" Miles asked. "Mr. Falco ID'd Hank, though."

"I know," Loralin declared. "I'm pretty sure he was mistaken. Do you have a current picture of Hank because his license picture from the employee file doesn't do him justice?"

Miles pulled a picture out of a file and handed it to his ex-wife. She then pulled a picture out of one of her files and set them side by side on Miles's desk. "Well, I'll be damned," he murmured. "Hank and Elijah look an awful lot alike."

"I was hoping they would," Loralin admitted. "I couldn't remember what Hank looked like because I was too far away when he was arrested. And the picture we took of his license when Devin hired him was just too grainy."

"So," Devin began. "You think Deke hired Elijah to kill Phyllis because she had been instrumental in his wife's injuries in the teaching hospital in Montana? Do you have any idea who killed Elijah?"

"My guess is Deke. I think Elijah was too sloppy and was always getting caught coming out of his room, so he did away with him."

"Could be," Miles said. "I'm going to have my officers investigate this stuff, and hopefully, if your hunch is correct, we can make an arrest soon. Of all people, you'd think Deke would be more careful."

"Yeah," Loralin agreed, but I think Phyllis's very public promotion may have set him off. So many people were triggered by it."

"True," Devin agreed. "So, what do you think is the reason Deke decided to stay with us all of a sudden? I highly doubt he visited his ex-wife every day from Casper."

"I'm guessing after the murder of Phyllis, he just wanted to keep an eye on Elijah and make sure nothing came back on him. And visiting his 'ex' was just a bonus. According to Don, he'd never loved anyone until Veronica appeared in his life."

"Okay then," Miles said as he moved to the door. "I'm going to go investigate this Montana teaching hospital and Elijah's connection to Deke. I'll let you know if we find anything."

Loralin and Devin followed Miles out. "Thanks," she said, hugging him.

"Don't thank me yet," Miles chuckled. "You can thank me when you turn out to be right, and we have a murdering snake in the grass in custody."

"Deal," she said, grabbing Devin's hand. "We're going to head home and get this hospital ick off of us."

"You do that," Miles said with a laugh. "I'll make sure to tell the girls to stay away for the day."

Devin laughed, and Loralin rolled her eyes. "You are cruising for a bruising," she told her ex.

"Do all old people talk like that?" Devin asked as they got into his car. "'Cruising for a bruising' makes you sound like you're a hundred years old."

"Well, according to you, I am." Leaning over in her seat, she kissed him and then kissed him again. "I love you, Devin."

"I love you too, Loralin."

* * *

By noon, Loralin was done with her work, so she decided to inspect the Inn. It was something she tried to do every couple of weeks. It was her way of making sure everything was running as it should.

The ground floor was all up to par. The lobby was filled with comfortable, clean seating and magazines and brochures to keep people busy. The self-serve coffee kiosks were all clean and running smoothly. Steven was good at making sure they never ran out of fresh beverages for people to have in the lobby.

The second through fourth floors were all cleaned, and the vending machines were full and in order. On her way down to the basement, she decided to stop by room 322 to see how it looked after the construction crews had finished a few days before.

"Looks pretty good, huh?" Loralin turned to see Lisa Marie standing there. "I was about to make sure it was clean and set out the welcome package. Guests are due today by two."

"It does look good," Loralin agreed. "I'm glad we can use it again."

"Me too," Lisa Marie said. "I always love it when we have a full house. It keeps us busy."

"Keep up the good work," Loralin said as she started to leave. But then she turned back. "Lisa Marie, I just wanted to say…"

"Not necessary, Loralin. We've known each other for a long time. And Devin and I weren't meant to be. I just hope you and he will realize soon that what you have is special and you're wasting precious years."

Loralin nodded and left the room. She'd wanted to apologize for coming between Lisa Marie and Devin, but in the end, it was better. She'd heard that the housekeeper was now in a steady relationship with the bartender who had given her an alibi after the last murder, so now they both had what they wanted.

Her next stop was the basement, where she checked on the boiler room and then the laundry room. The industrial washers and dryers were running at full capacity, and the person she'd hired to do the job was keeping the space clean and clutter-free.

As she walked toward the elevator, she decided to check the boiler room again. Something about it was bothering her since the basement was one of the places where Deke was seen with Elijah.

It took her a minute, but she finally realized what was off. There was a piece of white fabric just barely poking out from under the boiler. That was a fire waiting to happen, so she grabbed a long metal rod they used to push things into the boiler and swept the item out from under the machine. It was a hotel robe. Hadn't the killer been seen wearing one? Could this be it? Instead of touching it, she pulled out her phone and called Miles.

* * *

"What did you find, Loralin?" Miles asked as she led him and Henderson down into the depths of the basement. "I found a robe under the boiler. We're lucky it didn't cause a fire."

"Do you think that was Deke's plan?" he asked, just in case she hadn't given up the idea that he was out to destroy her.

"No. I mean, he could have put it there if he was involved with the murder, but I don't think he wanted the place to burn down while he was staying here. " Moving past Chloe, who had been guarding the door, she unlocked it and flipped on the light. The robe still lay there in the middle of the floor.

Miles put on some gloves and reached for an evidence bag that Henderson carried with her. "It's definitely a Robbin's Nest Inn robe," he said. "And it seems to have something red on the sleeve. I think we should get this to the lab as quickly as possible and see if we can find prints or blood or other evidence on it."

Henderson nodded and helped him bag the garment before turning and heading back out to her waiting cruiser.

"So, any news yet?" Loralin hazarded.

"No, not yet. But I'll let you know when I know."

"Thanks," Loralin said as she followed her ex-husband back up to the lobby. "I think I'm going to take Devin to visit his mother this afternoon. Tell the girls we won't be home until late."

Miles nodded and left the inn, while Loralin went in search of her manager. "Hey, do you want to go see your mum?"

"Yeah, that's probably a good idea. I need to keep my mind busy, or I'm going to sit here and wonder what is going on with the investigation." He looked like he was about ready to fly out of his skin.

"That's exactly why I suggested it. Besides, we leave for

Tasmania next week, so we don't have much time to get things in order." Loralin didn't know if she was more excited about the investigation or the trip.

They decided to take Loralin's SUV and were on the road by two thirty p.m. Visiting hours for that day were from four until six. They would make it just in time, then stop somewhere along the way home for a nice dinner.

"Are you nervous?" Loralin asked him. She figured he would be, if not outright terrified.

"Yeah, kinda scared," he admitted. "I know I have to do this, but I know that the way she looks at me when I tell her will make me feel like complete and total shit."

"Do you want me to come in with you?" She wasn't sure she'd even be allowed because of their history together, but she hoped she could. She wanted to assure Catherine Wentworth that she would take good care of her son.

"When I called and asked if you could come in, her therapist thought it might be good for her. But we won't be meeting in the normal community room. We will be in a secure room." Devin didn't seem to want to do anything but stare out the window. Usually, he'd be on his phone as she drove the hour and a half to the prison.

"Okay," she said softly. "If it starts to trigger her, I'll leave."

"That's fine," he said. "But at first, I think I need you in there with me." Loralin nodded and drove the rest of the way in silence.

* * *

Once at the prison, Loralin and Devin were shown into a room separated from a cubicle by thick glass. There were speakers and buttons on both sides so they could talk with Catherine.

"Hi, Mum!" Devin said as soon as she appeared in the room. "How are you?"

The woman sat down and looked between her son and Loralin. "As well as I can be in here. Did you bring the stuff I wanted?"

Devin nodded his head. "Yeah. The guards will give it to you when you go back to your cell."

"Thanks." It was a simple, quiet word that seemed to sap the energy right out of the woman. "So, Dr. Lovejoy said you needed to tell me something?"

"Yeah. Ummm, Mum, I just wanted to let you know that I love you and I'm sorry, but you were right about Loralin and me. We ignored it and fought it for years, but recently, we realized that we love each other."

The woman sniffed and looked directly at her son. "I told you. Maybe next time you will listen to your mum."

"Yeah," Devin said, unsure of where to go next. " So, uh, are you okay?"

"I'm good, dear," she said, looking at Loralin with a smile. "I don't agree with it. I don't think the age difference is appropriate, and the fact that you used be close to her daughter is troublesome… However, I know she makes you happy. Dr. Lovejoy has helped me see that. So as long as you are happy, there isn't much I can say about it." Her body slumped as if she'd just run twenty miles, but she kept the smile on her face.

"Thank you, Catherine," Loralin said. "I promise you that I love your son more than anyone on this earth, and I will make sure he is happy for as long as he'll let me."

The woman shrugged. "That's all a mum can ask for. Guard! I want to go back to my cell."

Devin thought about arguing and getting more time, but he didn't.

"Goodbye, Mum. I love you, and I'll see you as soon as we get back from Tasmania."

The guard entered the room and nodded at Loralin and Devin before he took Catherine's arm and led her from the room.

They got back into Loralin's SUV and headed west toward home. "Are you okay?" Loralin asked.

"Yeah," he said. "I guess I'm not used to seeing her so drugged up. I'm going to talk to her doctor and see if they can switch her meds. That's no way for her to live."

"I know. Do you want to stop for dinner or just head home?" she asked after a few minutes of silence.

"Can we just go home?"

Loralin nodded and pressed on the gas. They were about forty-five minutes outside of Elk River when her phone buzzed. It was Lisa Marie. "Hey, boss, Deke Robertson is running around here like a chicken with its head cut off. He's going to check out as soon as he can gather all of his stuff. I thought you should know."

"Thanks, Lisa Marie. You did well." She told Devin what was going on and pulled over to call Miles.

"This is Miles." He didn't sound the least bit grumpy. Could he actually be happy?

"Hey, Miles Deke is squawking and trying to check out. Do you think he saw us bring up the robe this morning? Do you think he knows his time is up?"

"He could," Miles admitted. And I just got some news that isn't going to look good for our friendly hotelier."

"Care to tell me what?" Loralin encouraged.

"Not yet. I'm still waiting for the final nail in his coffin. Can you keep him there?"

Loralin sighed. "I'm forty-five minutes away from the inn. I can try to have Maureen stall him during checkout and hope I get there with plenty of time to let you get the rest of your evidence."

"Okay," Miles said. "You do that, and I'll meet you at the inn within an hour."

When she hung up with her ex-husband, Devin was already on the phone with Maureen. She agreed to act like their system was down and delay checkout.

Loralin pulled back onto the road and pressed her foot to the gas. With any luck, the highway patrol wouldn't be out and about, and she could go ninety all the way home.

* * *

When Loralin walked into the inn, she saw Maureen alone at the desk. She hurried over to the young woman. "Is he still here?"

"Yeah," she said with a sigh. "He's waiting in the dining room. We offered him free food and drink."

"Perfect!" Loralin exclaimed. She headed for the dining room with Devin hot on her heels.

"Deke," she said as if nothing was wrong. "I hear you're finally leaving us."

"I would if your system wasn't broken," he said angrily. "How long does it take to fix that thing?"

"It all depends. I think the problem is with the server and not on our end." She kept her eyes on the man, not trusting him in the least.

Deke grumbled and took a sip of the alcoholic drink in his hand. If he was running away from the cops, he wasn't being very smart about it. "So, I've been meaning to ask you, are you and Jeremy related?" Devin cleared his throat, but didn't stop her like he wanted to.

"Who's Jeremy?" he asked.

"Oh, I'm sorry, you know him better as Elijah Montrose."

The man froze and looked between her and Devin. "I uh, I think he's a relative of someone from my past. He was a good kid. So sad that he was killed."

"Yeah," Loralin agreed. "I thought it was funny that he had the same last name as your ex-wife," she continued, baiting him.

"How did you know that?" he said, pushing his chair back and trying to stand.

"I know a lot about you that might surprise you," she said, holding his gaze.

"Then that means you know too much," he said, grabbing her by the arm and pulling her close to him. He easily thwarted Devin's attempt to reach her by kicking the table over and knocking him down.

"Let her go, Deke," Devin snarled. "You don't want to hurt her."

Deke laughed loudly. "She and her grandparents were always a thorn in my side. What does it matter now!"

Devin started walking slowly toward them until Deke reached under his jacket and pulled out a gun. In one swift movement, it was pointed at Loralin's head. "Stay back, and your girlfriend won't get hurt."

Devin stopped in his tracks, unsure of what he should do next. Where in the hell were Miles and the rest of the Elk River

PD? "Come on, man, you've already killed someone, don't add another body to the count."

"Shut up!" Deke raged. "I need to think."

Devin remained quiet, and when something caught his attention, he pretended he didn't see it. Miles and Sargent Henderson were coming in the back door of the dining room and slowly closing in on the man and his hostage.

"Deke Robertson put the gun down and stepped away from Loralin." The man jumped and turned around, losing some of his grip on Loralin. She and Devin took advantage of it. She fell to the ground while he pulled her to safety. If Deke hadn't been drinking, he might have gotten a shot off, but Miles and his men were on him before he could even think about it.

"Deke Robertson, you are under arrest for the conspiracy to murder Phyllis Palmer and the murder of Elijah Montrose. I'm sure the forensics from your gun will point the blame right at you."

Loralin was holding on tightly to Devin, and all she wanted to do was cry. "Is it over now?"

"It's over," Miles answered. "We found out that Elijah is the nephew of Deke's wife; they aren't divorced after all. She practically raised Elijah until Phyllis caused the injuries that sent her to a nursing home, and his biological father is the man who shot you. And we have a paper trail of money from Deke to your shooter and Elijah. It should be an open and shut case."

"What about the murder of Elijah?" Devin asked.

"The gun he held on Loralin is the same type that was used to murder Elijah. We're pretty sure that ballistics will match."

"And what about the robe we found?" Loralin asked as she started to get her feet back under her.

"There was a paper with Phyllis's room number and description in the pocket. It had both Deke and Elijah's prints on it. And the red stain was Phyllis's blood. Elijah had accidentally scratched her when they struggled. Plus, we are pretty sure the short brown hair found on the robe will match Elijah's."

"Damn, that was close," Loralin said as she took a seat at a nearby table and accepted water from Chef Pierre. "All of that last-minute evidence made the whole case. It was a good thing that the tests and forensics were rushed."

"You can thank our friend, Don," Miles said. "He is in good standing with the head of the state lab. He lit a fire under him."

Loralin laughed. "So, does that mean you won't quit if he comes here and takes over the chief position?"

"You know, it might make this department a bit more efficient to have someone who knows everyone in every law enforcement office in the state."

It wasn't an actual answer, but Loralin would take it.

Epilogue

Loralin settled into her seat on the plane as Devin did the same next to her. Heather, Hannah, Miles, Meredith, and her son Gabe Jr. were all in the rows behind them. It was finally time to leave Casper for a 25-hour-long trip to the land down under. "Are you excited?" Devin asked.

"You have no idea," she said as she leaned in and kissed him. Not just a quick kiss, but one that let anyone sitting near them know exactly what their relationship was.

It wasn't until Loralin pulled away from the kiss that she noticed the cheering from the people sitting behind them. "My family is so embarrassing," she chuckled. "I guess we aren't keeping it on the down-low."

"I guess not," Devin agreed. "And yeah, mine can be too."

"Speaking of which," Loralin said. "Where are Mark and Trevor?"

"They already left yesterday. They wanted to go get the hotel ready for everyone. My dad isn't too sure if my uncle has been running things properly. He's already sick of the business.

"Oh," Loralin said and went quiet, looking out of the small round window on the side of the plane.

"What's wrong?" Devin asked immediately. He knew her too well.

"I just... What if your dad wants to stay and take the hotel back? You might want to stay with him."

"Never," Devin said as he stood up out of his seat. "I was going to wait until we got to Tasmania, but it seems that my lady needs some reassurance." He got his carry-on bag out from the overhead bin and pulled out a small box. He opened the box as he got down on one knee. "Loralin Robbins. I love you more than anyone on this planet, and I can't even fathom spending my life with anyone else. Will you marry me?"

Another cheer went up from the family members behind them, and Loralin just smiled and stared at Devin. "Of course, I'll marry you. I… I love you so much."

Devin placed the ring on her finger and then sat back down in his seat just moments before the flight attendant announced that they would soon be taking off.

Loralin leaned over and kissed him. "Here's to the trip of a lifetime. And no murders. If there are any while we're gone, Maureen, Gage, Lisa Marie, Steven, Chef, Detective Henderson, and the new Chief, Don Peterson, will have to deal with it.

"Nah," Devin said with a smile. "No more murders for us. Here's to a new beginning for the future Mr. and Mrs. Devin and Loralin Wentworth."

As the plane lifted off the ground, Loralin smiled. "Now that sounds like the kind of life I want to live."

About the Author

JJ Weatherill is the author of 19 adult and young adult romance novels (JJ Ellis). She is a writer, graphic designer and long-distance mom to five kids. She enjoys reading, writing, graphic design, and watching cop shows on TV. She is having the time of her life writing cozy mysteries and can't wait to show you what's to come in the Robbin's Inn Mystery series. Grand Opening for Murder (book 1) and Promoted and Dead (book 2) are being published on the same day for the convenience of her readers. Book 3, A Death in Tassie, is coming soon! (Grand Opening for Murder was previously released under her original pen name of JJ Ellis but is no longer available for sale.)

www.ingramcontent.com/pod-product-compliance
Lightning Source LLC
La Vergne TN
LVHW021816060526
838201LV00058B/3408